# A STRANGE VOICE HAD AWAKENED HER

The eerie moonlight flooded the hallway where she stood, covering everything with a thin veil of translucent gauze. How strange everything seemed in this light. How unearthly the formal living room looked. The massive pieces of furniture crouched in the corners, as if waiting to spring out at her. She looked down the hallway toward the kitchen. It was a long tunnel of darkness—an endless tube of gloom that seemed to be drawing her forward. Almost against her will.

A sudden sound made her whirl around. Directly behind her, framed in the doorway, stood a tall figure dressed in a black cloak. A pointed hood shadowed the face, and only the large, burning yellow eyes were distinct. Sally was too frightened to make a sound. The figure raised a hand and pointed a long, bony finger at her. The voice was like a moan: "You are ours." As the words were spoken, the eyes of the creature grew in size and intensity, burning into Sally's soul.

It was only then that the strangled fear managed to wrench itself from her throat and escape as a horrified scream . . .

# THE DEVIL'S HOUSE

*by*
*Julia Tremonte*

PINNACLE BOOKS • NEW YORK CITY

THE DEVIL'S HOUSE

*Copyright © 1974 by Julia Tremonte*

All rights reserved, including the right to reproduce this book or portions thereof in any form.

An original Pinnacle Books edition, published for the first time anywhere.

ISBN: 0-523-00317-X

First printing, March 1974

*Printed in the United States of America*

PINNACLE BOOKS, INC.
275 Madison Avenue
New York, N.Y. 10016

# THE DEVIL'S HOUSE

# ONE

Sally Taylor stood in front of the mirror in the bathroom applying the last bit of makeup to her eyes. While she didn't ordinarily like to use cosmetics, today she wanted to look her best and she knew that just the right amount of color would bring out the brilliant blue of her eyes. When Sally had finished she stepped back a few paces and looked at herself. With her sweater thrown casually over her print blouse and her long, chestnut hair tied back with a blue ribbon, she looked more like a schoolgirl of seventeen than a married woman of twenty-three. But that was the effect she wanted and, taking a last look at herself, she walked out of the room, through the dressing area and into the living room.

Her husband Don sat on the couch flipping through the pages of an old magazine. He was three years older than Sally, but he still had the air of a clean-cut young man fresh out of college. They were an attractive couple; young, good-looking and still very much in love. It was almost a scandal with their friends the way they paid so much attention to each other, even at parties. While other couples separated and flirted harmlessly, Sally and Don were usually to be found in some quiet corner talking and laughing.

"It's positively obscene the way the two of you carry on," a friend had once said. "Don't you know it's against the rules to talk to your own husband in public?" Sally and Don had both laughed but they knew that theirs was the best way for them.

Looking up, Don threw the magazine carelessly on the coffee table and looked appreciatively at his wife. "Well, for all the time it took you, I expected a blonde or at least a redhead to confront me." He smiled his warmest smile, telling Sally that he liked the way she looked. "I could never understand why it takes a man five minutes to get ready and it takes a woman thirty."

Sally went and sat next to him, locking her arm in his. "Because, my darling husband, a woman has to look pretty and a man doesn't."

He leaned over and kissed her gently. "You look pretty all the time—but especially right now." Running his hand gently through her long hair, he asked seriously: "Are you scared?"

She smiled, but it wavered a little, showing the real emotion she felt inside. "I guess I am. But just a little. I never really thought of myself as a city girl before but now that we may be leaving I'm beginning to think that's what I really am." Her grip tightened on his arm.

"There are two things to remember, Sally. One is that we will be only a couple of hours from the city and two is that we have made no commitment on the house. You haven't even seen it, and if you don't like it then the question is settled: we'll stay here."

"I know," she said gently, "I'm being silly." Letting her eyes drift from her husband, Sally looked around the small East Side apartment they had lived in since they were first married. She had always thought of it as home. It was a comfortable, modern studio apartment in a high-rise building in one of New York's better neighborhoods. It had been Don's originally and they had kept it after they were married. While it was small for two people, Sally had made it charming and livable. But that was two years ago and things had changed. Don was making more money and they were now beginning to plan a family. They obviously needed something larger. But the thought of moving to the country had never occurred to her until he had mentioned it.

Don stood up. "I think that's time we get started. We have a long drive ahead of us." Seeing the forlorn look that crossed Sally's face, he laughed gently and said, "It's not that long a drive. We'll still be in the United States."

They locked the apartment, leaving one light on to discourage thieves, and took the elevator down to the garage. In less than ten minutes they were on their way toward the West Side Highway. It was a beautiful October day. The air was clean and crisp, the sun shone brightly in the cloudless sky, and there was a freshness to the day that was seldom felt. As they drove through Central Park Sally rather mournfully watched the people strolling with their children, the young couples walking hand in hand, the dogs running free and easy. Was she prepared to leave all this for the country? She laughed to herself. What she liked so much about the park was the fact that it reminded her of the country. But now that she actually had the chance to live where there were always trees and flowers, she was afraid. Why?

Driving up the highway with the river on one side and the once-fashionable Riverside Drive on the other, Sally considered what they were doing. Several weeks before, Don had seen an ad for a house for rent in upstate New York. Without telling Sally, he had taken the day off and gone there to inspect it. He had been full of elation when he returned that night. The house was perfect. It was furnished, located on acres and acres of land and was within commuting distance. He could live in the country and work in the city—the dream of many working men. Sally had been less than enthusiastic. She felt betrayed that he had not confided in her about his plans and that it seemed, in *his* mind at least, that they were ready to move. They rarely fought, but the episode brought on a flare-up that was only resolved when Sally agreed to see the house and to try to decide about it with an open mind.

That was a week ago and now they were on their way to the town of Anderson. The realtor had the keys and would show the house to the skeptical Sally. Backed up by her husband, he would try to sell Sally on the house. It was like a conspiracy. But at the same time she knew she was being unrealistic. Don really wanted the house. It was important to him and that should be important to her. She would find new friends, start a new life, have the baby they had so often talked about. It was selfish of her not to try to see it his way. And she knew that selfishness in a marriage was the beginning of the end.

As the car sped across the George Washington Bridge Sally turned back and looked at the towering skyline of Manhattan. What was so special about it?

In many ways it was beautiful, but in just as many ways it was a dangerous, ugly monolith that engulfed the people who lived there. To leave it would probably be a good thing; she had lived there long enough to become hardened toward the niceties of life, the everyday things other people took for granted. But still there was the fear lurking in the pit of her stomach. Was it because of the city? Or the country? Or was it something else?

"A penny for your thoughts," Don said, looking at her briefly.

"You'd be wasting your money. I was just thinking about you and me and New York and this house. I really am quite confused."

He let go of the steering wheel with his right hand and covered her left with it. Toying with her wedding band, he said, "Relax. Even if you don't like the house at least we've got out of the city for the day. Watch the scenery, breathe some fresh air for a change, enjoy yourself. I know a wonderful little inn that's on the way. We'll stop and have lunch there, that should cheer you up." He looked at her again, his eyes reassuring.

"That sounds like a good idea. I'm starved. You know I was so worried about this trip that I couldn't even eat breakfast. Now, I feel like I could eat a side of beef." It was true, the crisp air had made her ravenously hungry.

"If you don't watch out, you'll get fat." It was a joke of theirs. Sally was the trimmest girl he knew. She could eat anything without ever gaining a pound.

She squeezed his hand tightly. "I wouldn't mind getting fat ... if it were for a reason." She looked deeply into his eyes and felt his hand tighten on hers.

"Soon," he said. "Soon." But the expression on his

face had changed from one of playful solicitude to one of worry. Something in his manner made Sally wonder exactly what was going on in *his* mind.

The restaurant they ate at was called Molly's Inn and it dated from post-revolutionary times. Originally the home of a blacksmith, the inn was the main house connected by a recent addition to the forge room. It was here that Sally and Don ate, sitting in a booth that was once a horse's stable. The room was hung with antique harnesses, horseshoes, paintings, bellows and other things from the period and, across from them, the large fireplace was filled with an enormous, blazing fire.

"It's just like New York, isn't it?" Don asked with mild sarcasm.

"It's just beautiful. I never knew that places like this really existed. I always thought that they were dreamed up in the minds of Hollywood set designers."

"Not this place, it's the real thing. And," he hesitated, "only twenty minutes from Anderson. We could eat here often, make it 'our' restaurant. Of course there are others just as nice, but I think if *we* decide to move this should be where we come the most often." The waitress bringing their luncheon interrupted him.

How like a little boy you are sometimes, Sally thought. You've got to get your own way, no matter what. But, "It *is* nice here," was all she said before diving into her prime ribs of beef which she had ordered from the dinner menu at Don's insistence. "If you want a side of beef, then that's what you're going to get," he had said.

After lunch Don paid the bill and they got into the car to drive to Anderson, ten miles away. It was colder in that part of the state than it had been in the city and Sally pulled her sweater closer around her shoulders. What must it be like in winter? she wondered, thinking of Christmas card scenes of farmlands thickly covered with powdery white snow. It was already almost too beautiful to believe. The leaves had turned bright with vibrant colors; reds, yellows, golds, giving the whole countryside the look of an artist's palette covered with the pure colors straight from the tube. Somehow the leaves saddened the young woman. Their beauty was the beauty of death. In dying they made one last show of life, one last shower of glory before withering into brown refuse that littered the countryside. If only there wasn't death, she thought, looking stealthily at her husband. If only everything went on and on forever ...

Anderson was the smallest town Sally had ever seen. It was composed mainly of houses very much like the one which had become Molly's Inn. On the ground floor of many of the houses stores had been built instead of living quarters. In fact, the only modern building appeared to be a small supermarket which must have been built in the thirties and even that was in a colonial style. There was one main street flanked on either side by the houses, a small town square proudly flying the American flag above that of New York State and a large, white church. It looked more like a New England town than one in New York. Sally was charmed by everything. It must have shown on her face, for Don turned to her and said, "I knew you'd like it once you saw it."

He pulled the car into a parking space in front of a small, red saltbox-style house. A sign hanging above the front door said "Silas Dorn, Attorney at Law" in large, bold white letters. Underneath in a smaller, less obtrusive script, it read: "Justice of the Peace, Real Estate."

Catching Sally's look, Don said, "He's a jack-of-all-trades. In a town this size you have to be." He turned the powerful engine off.

"And master of none?" Sally asked innocently.

"New York sophistication, hah!" Don grunted in mock disgust. Quickly pecking her on the cheek he opened the door and got out, saying, "Wait here, I'll get Silas and we'll get going."

Sally watched the rugged form of her husband entering the small door of the office. Silas? she thought. On very friendly terms already. Well, Sally, you'd better like this place or you're going to be in for it. Through the bay windows of the office the young woman could see her husband talking with a man seated at a desk. After a minute he stood up and the two of them moved a little closer to the window and looked out toward where Sally sat. They were silent for a moment, then leaned their heads together and seemed to be whispering as if they feared she could hear them. That's odd, Sally thought. Unconsciously she ran her fingers through her hair, putting everything in place. She wanted to look her best for her husband's sake.

Eventually the door opened and Don and Silas Dorn stepped out into the sunlight. Dorn turned his back for a minute, locking the door, bending over to find the low keyhole. When he finally straightened up, Sally got her first good look at him. She immediately took a dislike to the man. It was irrational, but she couldn't help but respond to her immediate intuitions. But in all fairness, she thought, there have been very few people who have affected me like this.

Dorn stepped toward the car. He was a tall, thin man whose bones seemed to stick out through his clothing, giving him a very sharp, angular look. Sally noticed that his shoes were dirty. His face was thin. It narrowed from the back of his head like the blade of a hatchet. His skin was sallow and deeply pockmarked, the result of a childhood illness. The nose, which might have been called aquiline by a more poetic person, was ugly and hooked to Sally, who saw all his features as ugly parts of a grotesque whole.

Don reached the car first, opened the door and said, still outside, "Sally, this is Silas Dorn. He'll come in our car, it will be easier."

Sally turned her head away from Don and was confronted by Dorn's features pressed against the window next to her. She managed to keep her composure and rolled down the window. "It's a pleasure to meet you, Mr. Dorn," she said in her sweetest voice.

The man, who looked sixty from a distance, appeared to be in his mid-forties at a closer range. He thrust his hand through the opened window and took Sally's, which she proffered with some surprise, squeezing it in a limp, womanly fashion. His hand was moist and felt like the skin of a trout. "Likewise, I'm sure," he said, smiling and exposing two rows of yellowed and rotten teeth. His breath was fetid.

Don broke in. "Silas, if you'll get into the backseat, you can tell Sally all about the countryside on the way to the house." Don slid in next to his wife.

"No sooner said than done," the lawyer-realtor said, opening the back door. He sat leaning forward over the front seat between Don and Sally.

Don looked in the rearview mirror to see if there was any traffic before backing out. Seeing the face of Dorn staring directly at him, he said, "Silas, if you'd move your head I could see a little better." The man moved immediately.

As they drove out to the house, Sally had the strange feeling that her husband and this man were on more familiar terms than Don had said. Don seemed in charge of Dorn, which was very unnatural for people involved in a business deal—especially since it was Dorn who held the keys. For a second Sally felt like a stranger in the midst of friends. It made her heart go cold. How could Don know a man such as Dorn? Unconsciously she shook her head back and forth, thinking that it wasn't possible, that she was just being silly. But Don noticed the movement.

"Why are you shaking your head?"

"Just adjusting my hair, dear," she said lamely, feeling like a fool for having been caught off guard. "Tell me about the area, Mr. Dorn. It seems to be steeped in history." She wasn't really interested, but she needed a diversion.

"I'd be glad to Mrs. Taylor; glad to." Leaning forward, Dorn began to tell the history of Anderson and the surrounding towns. It was a fascinating tale and Dorn was a wealth of information.

Sally was half-listening, half-daydreaming as Dorn spoke. The sound of his voice, despite its sharpness, had a soothing quality that lulled her into a state of reverie. A pleasant warmth spread over her and it was with some surprise that she felt herself becoming sleepy. Blinking her eyes to keep awake, she scanned the countryside, deciding to savor the view. She saw that not only were the leaves in this part of the county not the brilliant colors that she had seen on the trip up, but they seemed to have died on the trees before falling. The landscape was a wash of shades of brown and gray. And there was something about the trees, the way they grew so close together that no sunlight penetrated to the ground, that struck her as peculiar. It was as if they were driving into a forest in the middle of the night instead of the middle of the afternoon. She shivered slightly, noticing how cold it had suddenly become.

Dorn's voice droned on. "And after the revolution the town, which had always been for independence, thrived. It was an agricultural community and because of the river nearby there was a great demand for its produce. It looked for a while like Anderson might become a real city." He sighed. "But then there was the industrial revolution in the North and our town seemed to get left by the wayside. As the big factories and farms in New England grew Anderson began to stand still. Then, gradually, it started to slip back. The people who once saw its future as bright and prosperous began to leave. There was a mass migration to the east and south to the city. That wasn't so long ago. Now we're just a commuter town, one of a string on the way to New York. It's sad in a way, but on the other hand, it keeps us a real community where everyone knows everyone else. There is a great deal of civic pride in our town which I think you'll grow to feel yourself."

There it was again, Sally thought. The assumption that *we* are going to live here. "Mr. Dorn, I'm sure that if Don and I decide to take the house we'll be just as much a part of the town as anyone else." She noticed Don frown at the tone of her voice and, not wanting to offend him, she added, "I really hope I like the house. Tell me all about it. What's its history?"

Dorn was silent. She could feel the pressure on the seat relax as the man sat back. After a few minutes he said, in an excited voice: "There's the Hendersons' house. They'll be your neighbors. They're a nice young couple, like yourselves. He's a consultant with some company in the city and spends a lot of his time up here. His wife is an artist—does beautiful things—and works at home too. I know you'll all get along. And just think, that will mean you'll have company while Don is in the city slaving away." He chuckled unpleasantly.

"So that's one fear down, Sally," Don said. "The fear of getting lonely while I'm away. There's even a path through the woods that connects the two houses." He reached out and patted her hand.

But Sally hardly heard a thing her husband said for she was staring out at the Henderson house in disbelief. It was set deep in the woods in a spot where almost no light reached its windows. But Sally was able to make out its general shape: there seemed to be turrets and cupolas, towers and porches, as if the designer had wanted to incorporate every possible style under one roof. It seemed to be made of wooden clapboard either painted gray or gone gray from neglect. The front door was windowed with stained glass and through it a bright light shone from somewhere deep within the house. There was no garden, in fact no lawn, just the wild creeping, growing things that crawled from the forest to tangle themselves around the base of the house. The trees around the house, pines and spruces—not the oaks and elms of the remaining countryside—swayed back and forth in a strong breeze. But everywhere else the trees were calm.

Her eyes were riveted on the Henderson house. She even turned her head backward to watch it fade into the gloom. A feeling of deep disgust coursed through her body, settling in the pit of her stomach and making her feel slightly sick. What was it about that house that brought on such a strong reaction? She didn't know, and she prayed to God that she never found out.

"Sally? Sally?" Don's questioning voice brought her back to reality. "What's the matter with you. You haven't been listening to a word I've said." Looking at her sternly he noticed something. "You don't look well. Do you feel all right?"

She forced a smile. "I'm just a little tired and nervous. And it's so stuffy in here." Rolling down the window brought in a rush of icy air, heavy with the scent of autumn and forest. It instantly revived her. "Do we have much farther to go?" The question sounded like a plea.

"Perfect timing," Don said, "we're here." He slowed the car and turned off the road to the left.

They drove through an ancient stone gateway whose ornate, iron gates lay rusted on either side and onto a deeply rutted road that twisted and turned away from the direction they had come. It was a bumpy ride and Sally clutched the door handle to steady herself. The forest here was much like everywhere else. The trees were covered with dead leaves and the passage of the car by them caused a flurry of activity as they detached themselves and tumbled to the ground. It was dark and gloomy. Sally unsuccessfully strained her eyes to see the sun. The air she had minutes before found so refreshing was now too cold.

"It's not so bad, once you get used to it," Dorn said, noticing that Sally had closed her window again.

Sally didn't know whether he meant the cold air or the darkness that seemed to prevail. It didn't matter for she thought that she'd never get used to either.

The road twisted farther and farther away from the main road toward the house. It seemed to Sally that they were getting deeper and deeper into the abysmal forest, when suddenly the trees gave way and a clearing appeared. Don pulled the car up just at the rise of the hill and said, "We'll walk from here. I want you to get the feel of the grounds and see the view. It's breathtaking."

The three people got from the car and began the walk. Once they were in the clearing, the sun broke through and bathed everything in a bright, harsh light. Sally visored her eyes with her hand and looked around. The difference between the forest and where she now stood was astounding. She could feel the warmth touching her skin; almost grasp the yellowness of the mid-afternoon sun. The clearing was the light at the end of a long, dangerous tunnel and Sally was relieved to be standing there.

Taking a quick look around, the young woman realized that they were standing on top of a small mountain surrounded on all sides by a forest that stretched off in every direction. They stood on the bald spot of the crown, and in the center of this was the house. Sally had hardly noticed it because she was so overwhelmed by the view. But once her eyes rested on the house they stayed there, fascinated.

At first glimpse, Sally's heart jumped because she thought she was seeing a duplicate of the grotesque Henderson house; but she had been wrong. While the style was very similar—an abundance of fancy woodwork, turrets and porches—the house itself was much more welcoming. It was painted a bright, pure white, with a pale green trim, so pale, in fact, that it appeared to be off-white. Instead of a tangle of weeds and vines clawing at the house, there was a garden that extended around the front and sides, adding a splash of color to the yard. The last of the hearty plants added accents of color to the front of the porch, with their yellows, reds and oranges. The lawn, still green, was carefully trimmed and the hedges carefully clipped. It was a picture-book house in a picture-book setting.

Sally whirled around and looked at her husband, who was standing just behind her. "Don, it's lovely. I don't think I've ever seen anything so beautiful."

He moved up to her and put his arm around her. "I knew you'd like the house ... you had to." He squeezed her tightly. "Why don't we go inside? It's even more beautiful. I don't know who furnished or designed the house, but they certainly had good taste. But you'll see." He propelled her forward to the porch steps then halted, turning toward the realtor, who was staring out into space. "Dorn, we'll need the key to get in."

The man's reverie was broken as the words reached his ears. "The key?" He looked puzzled. "You won't need a key, the door's not locked." His scarecrowlike figure started toward them. "No reason to lock up, no one ever comes around here." Seeing the look in Don's eyes, he hesitated. "We never have any trouble with people getting broken into, that's all. No one around here locks their doors. No need to." He began to move closer to the house.

"In that case, why don't you wait for us outside? I'd like to show Sally around myself."

"Anything you say. It's your house," he said taciturnly, going back toward the car.

Sally picked up on his words. "What did he mean by that?"

Don took hold of her by the shoulders and looked

her straight in the eyes. "This house means more to me than anything I've ever wanted—except you. It is a place where we can live away from the city and its dangers, a place where I can love you in peace and quiet, and a place where I can be the father that I've always wanted to be." Her look softened. "I know we've always talked things out before doing anything that concerned the two of us, but in this case I felt sure that you would love the house as much as I did, so I put down a deposit when I was here before." His fingers tightened on her shoulders.

Sally drew back. "You took the house before I had a chance to see it? Don, why? Suppose I don't like it. Don't you realize that you're forcing me. Why didn't you tell me all this before? I feel like I'm being taken advantage of." With a sharp motion she pulled his arms from her body and walked away.

"Taken advantage of? By your own husband?"

She stopped in front of a large stained-glass window, looking at her reflection in a piece of red heart-shaped glass. The youthfulness of the morning was gone; her face looked drawn and tired, her hair blown askew by the wind. "Yes," she said sadly, "by my own husband."

Don stood for a moment, watching her standing like a little girl whose pet kitten was missing. It infuriated him when she looked like that. Without another word he stepped from the porch and called to Dorn. "Silas I'm afraid I've made a mistake. We won't be taking the house after all, my wife doesn't like it." The man in the distance just stared. Don strode across the porch and took his wife roughly by the wrist. She just stared at him in surprise. "Well, don't just stand there looking like a wooden Indian. You want to go, so we're going." He dragged her toward the steps of the porch.

Sally's voice filled the cold air with pain. "Don, what's come over you? You're hurting me. Let go." She felt herself trembling but was unable to control it. What *had* come over her husband? She had never seen him act like this before ... toward anyone, certainly not toward her. She wrenched herself away from him. "You're acting like a madman, stop it." Her voice was firm, though her legs were like rubber. The sun was starting to set in the distance and the air grew cold as the light began to fail. "If you'll just give me a chance, I'd like to see the house for myself and make up my own mind."

Don stood before her, his face drained white from emotion. He had never let his anger, his sometimes uncontrollable anger, get the better of him in front of his wife ... except this time. He immediately regretted it. He stood for a minute watching his wife enter the house, then quickly followed her. She was standing in the entrance foyer looking like a child in a candy store. With two steps he was at her side. Leaning forward, kissing her neck, he said softly, "I'm sorry, darling. It's just that I want everything to be right for us."

Sally was so distracted by the house that she hardly realized what her husband was talking about. In a very distant voice she said, "I understand." She walked away from Don into the first room to her left. Don smiled inwardly.

The main living quarters of the house were on two levels. There were also an attic and cellar, though they weren't equipped for occupants. From the entrance foyer a long hallway ran through the house to the back and the kitchen. Off this hallway, in the foyer, was the formal living room that had been carefully decorated and contained two couches, several chairs and many paintings and etchings. The predominant color was yellow, which made the room bright and cheerful. An enormous fireplace took up a great deal of space on one wall and Sally could picture the winter nights when she and Don might sit in front of a fire, talking.

Directly behind this room was a smaller, less formal room, which Sally took to be the dayroom or den. It had built-in bookcases and a large desk, as well as several comfortable-looking chairs. The tall windows of this room looked out over the valley below. This room also had a fireplace and she knew that it would be here that they would spend most of their time, for it was so comfortable, so pleasant and inviting. And besides, it led directly into the kitchen and if she knew anything about her husband he would want to be as close to the food as possible.

She walked into the kitchen and gasped. In the city she was used to a reconverted closet which was laughingly called a kitchen. Now, Sally stood in the middle of a room the size of her New York living room. The stove, modern and gleaming white, stood against one wall; the refrigerator, also new, stood against the other. But where were the washing facilities? The open door to her left led to the dining room. She stepped gingerly around the large kitchen table and found a second door that opened into a pantry lined with cupboards, marble-topped counters, a sink, and a dishwasher. It was the most beautiful kitchen she had ever seen in her entire life.

By the time Don found her she was practically doing pirouettes. "Oh, Don it's so beautiful I can't believe it." His smile was self-satisfied. "All right, Mr.

Smart Guy, you don't have to look so smug. So you were right, so what?" she laughed gaily.

"I'm not looking smug. I'm just thanking myself for having married you and having got to know you so well that I can tell what you like and what you don't like. Believe me, I'm not trying to crush your ego with mine."

Sally squeezed his hand. "I know that. It's just that sometimes it's hard living with someone else and being able to keep your own identity. You understand." Her eyes caught sight of another door. She broke away from her husband. "And where does this mysterious door lead to?" Her hand was on the knob when Don stopped her.

"Just the cellar. But you'd better not go down there, the stairs need repairing and I'm afraid you'll hurt yourself." His face wore a look of concern.

"All right," she said, taking his hand playfully, "but now you're going to have to show me the rest of the house, sir."

"I'd be delighted, my lady," Don said, joining in the spirit of the game. "If you'll just follow me." He led her out of the kitchen into the hallway, then to the front of the house and up the narrow stairway to the second floor. "You're going to like this part of the house, I know."

He was right. The second floor was composed of three large bedrooms and one smaller one. Every room had a view of the valley below; the master bedroom was particularly splendid with wide, tall windows looking over the countryside. This room, the one that would be theirs if they took the house, was done all in rose, pale and shimmering in the afternoon sunlight. Heavy drapes flanked the windows and the bedspread matched their deep red hue.

Sally walked quietly around the room, examining everything in sight. Don stood by the door, watching her silently. This would be the moment of truth. He knew somehow that if his wife liked this room she would like the whole house, and he was almost certain that she would. Sally turned after a minute and said, "Don, this room is beautiful. In fact, the whole house is just what I always hoped we would find. Let's take it." She moved toward him.

"We'll take it on one condition. And that is that you really do want to live here; that you're not just saying it to make me feel happy." He studied her seriously.

She smiled slightly. "You know me better than to think that I would do something like that. It would be dishonest and, sooner or later it would be a block between us. No, I love the house and want to take it. I know we'll be happy here." Quickly, without saying another word, she threw her arms around her husband and kissed him, happier than she had been in many months. "Let's find that creepy real estate agent and tell him we want the house, he looks like he could use some good news."

At the top of the stairs Don stopped her once again and said, "Are you absolutely certain you want to live here? You know it's going to be much different from living in the city."

"I'm positive. And, I'm sorry I acted foolishly before. I was nervous, I guess." Her sense of betrayal faded away as she thought of how she would rearrange the furniture in the house and add little touches of her own. It was as if her whole life were going to start anew.

Don smiled. "Don't worry about it. I know it's a big step for us and I can appreciate how you felt. Come here." He pulled her close to him and kissed her for a long time. Sally heard a noise from below them and opened her eyes for a brief moment to see what it was. Standing at the foot of the stairs, watching the couple with a look of evil satisfaction stood Silas Dorn. Sally felt a wave of fear and loathing rush through her body. All too suddenly this horrible man had begun to play an important role in her life—their life—and she wondered just how important that role would become.

# TWO

They moved into the house just before Christmas, just before New York City launched itself into its frantic Christmastime excess. Despite the bright lights and the fabulous store decorations along Fifth Avenue, the ice skating at Rockerfeller Center, the warmly bundled men selling roasted chestnuts and the electric quality of the cold winter air, the city had an atmosphere of greed and selfishness. There was a fast-running current of mercantilism that pushed people to spend more than they could afford, see people they really didn't want to see and go places they never would have visited on any other occasion.

This was the side of the city that Sally had always hated. And this is what she was glad to be getting away from. The memory of the gray slush in the streets, the cold winds whipping down through the great cavernous canyons of the city were just that: memories. That had all been replaced by the countryside with its miles and miles of snow-covered trees and small houses with narrow ribbons of smoke pouring from the chimneys, the little towns and country stores, the friendly faces and the heartfelt best wishes for the holiday season. It was a joy to be away from the city and in the country.

Don had driven back to see Silas Dorn the following weekend to sign the papers. The rent was amazingly cheap and Sally questioned the reason for this. In fact, she thought it rather odd that the house was vacant at all; it was so lovely. Apparently Dorn had no explanation for this. When she asked Don the reasons, he merely shrugged his shoulders. Still, something in the back of her mind nagged at her about the house. On the other hand, with the moving and the new joy she felt, there was little time for Sally to be skeptical. She thanked her lucky stars for her new house and for her husband whom she was growing to love more and more with each new day.

Don had taken a week of his vacation in order to move and, with the week he got from the company for the holiday, he had two full weeks off. Because the house was furnished, they decided to sell their furniture, keeping only what they really needed or what had some sentimental value, and move into the house afresh. It was a wonderful feeling to be able to almost completely turn their backs on the life they had led before and look forward to an entirely new way of life. Don, for the first time since they had been together, began to seriously think of leaving his job and setting up his own business to be run from the house. As an architect he could work almost anywhere, if he could get the business, and considering that he had a particular interest in the restoration of old houses, he felt that there might be a good chance for him to be able to work right in the vicinity.

Sally also began to think of things she had always

hoped for. The most important thing in her mind was the baby. She had already decided she wanted a boy so Don would have a son. She wanted a girl herself, but that could wait for a few more years, the son would come first—she had always known that. The years of putting off a family for reasons of space in their cramped apartment, of Don's trying to get himself established at his job, and the thousand other reasons one can find in the city for not doing something, were all behind them now. With the house, the land, and all that new freedom, they could finally start to become a real family.

"Do you have to go back to the city, Don?" Sally asked one bitterly cold morning several days before Christmas. He had sprung the news on her rather unexpectedly over breakfast. It had started off as a perfect day with the pale sun rising over the white landscape, the two of them wrapped around each other in the warmth of their slow lovemaking, oblivious of the outside cold. They had raced quick-footed over the cold wooden floors to get dressed, and leisurely eaten an enormous breakfast in the dining room.

Don took Sally's hand. "I'm afraid that I have no choice. There was something that came up yesterday at the office and I had the bad fortune to call in to see how things were going. I shouldn't have called, but it's too late now. I'll only be gone for two days—three at the most. You'll be all right here, won't you?" His fingers tightened on her hand.

"Of course I'll be all right, it's just that I'm going to miss you. You know it's not like being in the city. I don't have anyone I can call, or anywhere I can go."

"If that's what's worrying you why don't you come

with me? We can check into a hotel and . . ." He never finished, for Sally quickly interrupted.

"I didn't give up the city just to go running back to it. No, I'll stay here; there's a lot to be done yet. I'm sure I'll keep myself busy."

Don wasn't convinced. There was a hesitation in his wife's voice. "If you're really worried, I can call Silas Dorn and see . . ."

Sally's reaction was something between a laugh and a cry. "Don't do me any favors. If I want to see any spooks, I'll turn on the horror movie on television. I still think there's something very strange about that man. Something very strange indeed."

Don laughed. "I think that you had better stop watching those movies. Silas Dorn just happens to be a little peculiar. It's probably from living up here all his life."

"And is that the way we're going to end up after a few years? Like a spook looking for a house to haunt?"

"Well, if it is, you're going to be the best-looking spook the spirit world has ever seen." He leaned across the table and kissed her gently on the forehead. "Now, I've got to go. I promise I'll call you every night. And, I'm sorry about the car." Train service from the town to the city had been disrupted, as frequently happened, and would not be in service until the next day. Consequently, Don was forced to take the car into the city, leaving Sally by herself in the house. Luckily, they had plenty of food stocked.

"Don't worry about me, I'm a big girl now. I can take care of myself."

"I know you can but just the same, be careful. Make sure the doors are all locked every night and don't go out after dark—there are still wild animals around here and I don't want to come home to find you in little pieces."

Sally got up from the table. "You'd better go or you'll be late. I'll walk out with you."

A few minutes later, they stood on the snow-covered driveway holding hands. A strong, cold wind blew in from the valley and rustled the dry, dead branches of the trees. A few small brown birds pecked at the frozen ground, looking for food. The plaintive whine of a sawmill in the distance filled the air with sorrow. Don left with just a quick "good-bye," heading the car down the treacherously icy driveway toward the main road. Trembling softly from the cold, Sally stood still for a few minutes, until the car was out of sight. When she was sure that Don had safely reached the road she turned, feeling lost suddenly, and went back into the house to do the breakfast dishes.

That night she heard the noise for the first time. It was ten o'clock. Sally had turned on the television, hoping that the news would keep her mind off the fact that she was alone. She and Don had decided that the smaller of the two living rooms, the one that was like a study, would be the ideal place for the television as well as all their leisure activities. Don had stacked logs for the fireplace before he had left and now they were burning fiercely, warming the room and Sally's spirits. She hated to be away from her husband, especially since she was now virtually cut off from any form of communication with the outside world.

With the lights off and the fire crackling loudly over the humdrum voice of the announcer, the room was pleasant enough. And Sally, wrapped in a warm blanket, more for comfort than a defense against the cold, was snuggled up in a large chair. The noise started halfway through the news. At first it sounded as if something in the television itself were about to break. There was a low, moaning sound which rose and fell in pitch, like a sob.

Cursing the modern practice of making products that broke only weeks after they had been bought (for the television was only a month old) Sally got out of her chair and tried to adjust the volume. Nothing she did had any effect on the sound. In fact, even when she had turned the sound off the moaning continued. Finally in desperation, she turned the television off completely. The sound stopped instantly.

Fifteen minutes later, after she had picked up a book to while away the time before she went to bed, the sound began again. This time it was louder and stronger. The hairs on the back of her neck rose as she realized that it was not coming from the television set after all, but from somewhere inside the house. With trembling hands she set the book down in her lap as quietly as possible and listened to the noise.

It could have been a human voice in pain, or it could have been the sound an animal makes before it is about to attack; a low moaning growl. Sally could not determine what was making the sound, only that it was nearby and getting louder by the minute. A quick glance around the room showed no source that was within her range of vision. She had remembered to close and lock all the doors—she had even locked all the windows as Don had instructed her. It was not possible that something—or someone—had got in, yet the horrible sound was coming from within the house.

How could something have gotten in? she wondered, trembling now from fear rather than the cold.

Then it occurred to her that she had not gone into the cellar to check the windows there. In fact, she had *never* been in the cellar—Don had said that the stairs were dangerous. That must be the answer. Something was trapped down in the cellar. Something that wanted to get out. She had to know.

Despite her fear, Sally rose from the chair, put down her book and walked into the kitchen, being careful to turn on the light. She went immediately to the pantry and got the carving knife from its place in the drawer and returned to the main room and stared at the cellar door. The noise, that awful animal noise had stopped. Had whatever it was in the cellar heard her moving around? At that moment it didn't matter. Wondering what was underneath the house more than fearing to face it, Sally opened the cellar door. A rush of damp, fetid air assailed her nostrils, forcing her to take a step or two backward. Barely able to control herself, the young girl retraced her steps. Breathing through her mouth, she found the light switch on the stone wall to her left and turned the lights on.

The cellar was barely illuminated by a pale, sickly light: I shouldn't be doing this, it's dangerous, Sally kept telling herself. At the same time, a compelling force kept her moving. She placed a foot on the top step and began to descend. After what seemed hours, she reached the floor of the cellar. This room, the foundation of the house, was carved out of a heavy, gray rock that oozed moisture and supported a veritable jungle of slimy-looking moss. The room appeared empty, for the naked lightbulb illuminated only a small circular area in the center of the room.

Sally stood at the bottom of the stairs, knife in hand, staring around her. There was not a sound in the room, with the exception of water trickling from the rocks on the floor of the cellar. A thought suddenly flashed through her mind: there was nothing wrong with the stairs, they were not dangerous. Why had Don said they were? Was it to keep her away from the cellar? Why would he do something like that?

As her eyes grew accustomed to the dark, Sally was able to make out some shapes she had not noticed before. In a corner stood something which looked like an old washtub. Next to it was a broken rocking chair. At the far end of the room there seemed to be a large pile of rocks.

Her eyes went to the windows. There were only two, and they were both shut—boarded up, in fact. The noise she had heard must have been the winter wind blowing in from the outside, shrieking as it forced its way through the cracks between the wooden frame. Relieved, she smiled and began to climb the stairs.

The stairs were the old-fashioned kind; planks nailed across a grooved beam. They were merely steps without a backing. As Sally made her way toward the kitchen once again, her eyes caught the sight of something moving in a far corner of the cellar. Through the slats of the stairs she saw something tall and black step from the shadows into the room. It almost looked like a man, but she couldn't be sure. Fear engulfed her now, and she raced to the top of the stairs into the kitchen, and locked the door. Her entire body was shaking from fright as she realized for the first time that she was not alone in the house.

Someone—or something—was waiting for her in the cellar.

The last thing she remembered was the moaning sound starting again and the sound of something moving closer and closer toward her.

# THREE

When Don returned the next day in the late afternoon, he found Sally in bed in their room, with the door locked. It didn't take many questions to find out from the terrified young woman what had happened. At first Don seemed concerned, but as Sally began filling in the details of what had happened, a rather skeptical smile etched its way across his face.

When she had finished, he said, "Sally, I don't like this. I think you let yourself get overtired from working around the house. We're going to be here for quite some time, you know. There's no need for you to try to get everything done all at once, it's not good for you." His voice was soothing and reassuring, but Sally was offended by the mere idea that what had happened to her might have been imagined.

Her face colored and she spoke angrily. "Stop treating me as if I were a child. You know as well as I do that I do not have an overactive imagination and I never have. Whatever it was that I saw in the cellar was there!"

Don realized his mistake. His wife was much too intelligent to be treated like a little girl. Running his fingers through her long hair, he said, "I'm sorry, darling. It's just that I would rather think that you imagined everything than that you were really in any danger here last night. If you want, I'll go down in the cellar and look for myself."

Sally softened. "Would you? Although I don't know what good it will do, whatever it was has probably gone." She watched as her husband left the room and went to investigate her story. She had meant to ask Don why the stairs to the cellar were not in disrepair, as he had said, but in the excitement of his return, she had forgotten.

When he returned ten minutes later, his face was grim. "Sally, I don't know whether I should be happy to tell you this or not, but I couldn't find anything down there. You know that the cellar hasn't been used in years and it's covered with a thick layer of dust. I checked everywhere and I couldn't find any trace of footprints of either a man or an animal."

Sally was silent. Maybe her husband didn't believe that she had seen something beneath the house, but she knew that she had. Of that she was positive.

The incident was forgotten during the next few days as the couple began to prepare for the Christmas holiday. They had decided that they would spend the season alone together, not inviting any of their city friends up. Next year maybe, but this time they wanted to be alone. The day before Christmas Don received a phone call. When he had hung up, Sally questioned him apprehensively, afraid that he might have been called in to the city again. She didn't want to be alone in the house.

"You can take that look off your face, young lady,

I'm not going anywhere. That was Ralph Henderson, our nearest neighbor. You remember. Dorn pointed out their house to us when we first came up here. He said that he'd like us all to get together, considering we're the only four people for miles around, so I suggested they come over tonight for a drink. Don't worry, they won't stay long." He scooped her into his arms. "We'll have the entire evening together; just the two of us."

"I'm glad you asked them over. I've always wondered what kind of people could stand to live in a house like theirs ... it was monstrous. I can still see it sitting in that forest of dead trees." A shiver ran through her body.

"You may think so, but I have an idea that they like it that way, so for heaven's sake, don't let them know how you feel. Besides, you may be surprised to hear that the same man who designed their house designed this one. They're practically the same, if you take the time to look."

Sally was curious. Don acted as if he knew these people already, since he knew that they liked the house, and knew who had designed it. An icy feeling clutched at her heart. She felt exactly as she had the day she had seen Don and that awful man Dorn together. They seemed to know each other, to be friends, when he protested that he had only met the realtor the week before. Why would Don hide all this. "How do you know about their house?" she asked as innocently as possible.

"Oh, that. When I was deciding about this house I looked up the records in the county files and noticed the similarity in styles. A little checking gave me the answer." He stopped suddenly and his nose wrinkled up. "Do I smell something burning?"

"My biscuits," Sally shrieked. She fled to the kitchen, forgetting about neighbors, houses and architects.

An hour after Sally and Don had finished washing the dishes—which consisted of loading the dishwasher, which had become indispensable—the doorbell rang. Don went eagerly to answer it. For a minute Sally sat alone in the back room watching the tongues of fire lick the smoldering, crackling logs. Somehow, with the ringing of the bell she felt that her life was about to change. It was a feeling which sprang from deep inside her, uncontrolled and unwanted. It was as if the ringing of the doorbell was the death knell for a part of her life with Don that she would never again be able to recapture. Why she had these thoughts she did not know, why she was certain of them she also did not know. She only knew that since they had moved to the house things had begun to happen to them; they had been caught up in something that started with the figure in the cellar and would end with . . . what?

"And that pensive character sitting by the fire is my wife, Sally. She rather looks like she fell out of a Dickens' novel; poor little waif." Don had entered with the guests while his wife had been deep in thought.

Sally suddenly realized the picture she must be making for the three of them. Embarrassed, she got to her feet and looked at the guests. "Winter nights in front of the fire always make me feel a little sad. How do you do, I'm Sally Taylor." She walked toward the three, her hand extended.

The other woman stepped forward and took Sally's hand. "Hello, I'm Evelyn Henderson, and this is my husband, Ralph." The man nodded, smiling. The woman was in her early thirties and dressed very much in the country way. She wore a simple knit dress of black, which could have easily been handmade, a small rhinestone brooch in the shape of a Christmas tree and tiny earrings to match. Her shoes were a year or so out of style and the bolero jacket, also knit, carelessly thrown about her shoulders completed the picture. She was definitely not headed for the pages of Vogue. When she spoke, her voice was heavy and almost masculine, caressing in a most intimate and disconcerting manner. "You know, Sally, I always find that fire has quite the same effect on me. It's something about the collective unconscious; the common inheritance of man. The fascination with flames and heat is common to everyone." She smiled and her eyes glowed in the firelight.

"Either that, or it's just a throwback to the animal beginnings where it meant warmth and protection," Ralph said. He was dressed very casually in a plaid hunter's shirt and heavy, baggy trousers that gave him practically no shape at all. His voice, though scholarly, was rather tentative, as if he expected someone to immediately contradict him. Someone did.

"Nonsense, Ralph," Evelyn said. "Everyone knows that animals are afraid of fire. Man is the only animal that seeks out his warmth and protection." She stared at her husband, waiting for him to answer.

"And man is the only animal that kills for no reason other than the sheer pleasure of killing." He glared back at his wife.

Don interrupted and stopped what seemed to be the beginnings of a fight between the two visitors. "Can I get anyone a drink?" he offered. Everyone accepted and when the four were seated, Sally turned to Evelyn.

"Don't you ever get lonely or afraid out here in the country? Or, have you gotten used to it?"

Evelyn sipped her drink, then answered. "Ralph has the good fortune to be home most of the time—he's a consultant, you know—so it's very seldom that I am ever alone. As for being lonely, it's out of the question. I savor the moments I have by myself, they're all too few. I am not the kind of woman who is afraid of many things. I have lived in this part of the country all my life and there are very few things that can make me afraid ... very few indeed." Her smile was quizzical.

Ralph was quick to chime in. "My wife is the most fearless woman I have ever encountered. She'd run after a wild animal if she thought it had taken something that belonged to her."

Evelyn hardened. "I'd run after anything if I thought it had taken anything of mine ... anything. But why do you ask, dear?"

Sally didn't like to be called by this familiar term. Not because it inferred a relationship closer than the one she had with the other woman, but because it made her seem a child who was being addressed by an older, more knowledgeable person. Sally said, "It's just that I had a very odd experience the other night while Don was in the city, and it suddenly occurred to me that I was totally alone out here. If something happened, there would be no one to turn to."

"But Sally, you could always turn to us. There is a direct path linking this house with ours. If anything happened, all you would have to do is to call us on the telephone and Ralph and I would be here in no time. But tell me," she said, full of curiosity, "what happened the other night."

Don cut in. "But you don't want to hear that story."

Evelyn stopped him cold with a statement that was more like a command. "Oh yes I do, and I can tell that Sally is just dying to tell us, aren't you?" She leaned forward in her chair and spoke the words softly.

Sally noticed the intensity in the woman's green eyes, the deep shadows that seemed to lurk there, the imploring that was not to be denied. Feline, she decided. Her eyes are feline. In fact, she had carried herself like a cat when she walked into the room, sniffing out the situation, looking into corners. Now Sally had to tell her story to this woman against her husband's wishes. They would have an argument later, but it was too late now. So she told the company the entire story. When she had finished, she waited for their reactions.

Evelyn smiled and said, "And you actually took a knife and went down into the cellar, not knowing what you might find? That was very brave." She turned a steely eye toward her host. "You have a very strong, very brave wife, Donald. I hope you know that."

Don's face was drawn. He looked uncomfortable. "I've known it for a long time." As if to change the subject, he asked if anyone wanted another drink. When they agreed, he refilled the glasses and said, "Now, as our first guests and, considering that it's Christmas Eve I want you—Evelyn and Ralph—to put an ornament on our tree as a sign of friendship and good luck—for all of us."

"Of course, Donald," Ralph said. "What a good idea."

As they moved into the more formal room where the tree had been set up, Sally again had the feeling that the three others knew each other. This time it was so strong that she felt as if she were an outsider in a group of friends. The way they had both called her husband "Donald" had betrayed a closeness that a few minutes conversation could not have developed. And there was almost a sound of approval when Evelyn had noted how brave she was. Could they have all known each other before and not be letting on? It was insane, but the feeling still rested uneasily with Sally.

"What a beautiful tree," Evelyn said. "I imagine you cut it yourself. There's really no point in paying for one when we have these lovely forests around us." She moved closer to the tree and was bathed in its twinkling red lights. "Such a warm feeling, so much like the fire, don't you think." Before anyone had a chance to answer, she went on. "It's very strange when you think that the Christmas tree is not really a Christian concept. That is it is more a concession to the old gods, to the pagan gods than something that Christianity brought about. How strange that people who believe in God and trust in him should have a pagan symbol, the very symbol of the devil, in their homes at the highest holiday in the Christian faith. I've always thought it was rather blasphemous. Now where are the ornaments?"

She took one that was offered and carefully put it on the tree. "Although I must say that a pagan symbol in this house is more than appropriate, don't you think, Ralph?"

Sally saw the man tense and clench his teeth. "Sometimes, Evelyn, you talk too much." He snatched the ornament from his wife and tied it haphazardly to the tree.

Suddenly Sally felt scared. What was she talking about? She looked at her husband, but his face was blank. Ralph was red and obviously angry. Evelyn looked as if she had let the cat out of the bag and was enjoying every minute of it. Sally was growing to dislike the woman. "Evelyn what did you mean by that? Why should this house have anything to do with pagans?"

The other woman looked surprised. "Why, my dear, I haven't frightened you, have I? I thought that by now Donald would have told you all about this house." She coyly sipped her drink.

Sally turned on her husband, feeling so completely left out and frustrated that she was sure that if someone didn't start explaining things to her she would begin crying. "Don, what are they talking about?" Her shaky voice betrayed her emotions.

"There's no need for you to get upset, Sally. It's all in the past. I'll tell you later." He moved to put his arms around her, but she rejected them.

"I want you to tell me now, since I am the only one who doesn't know about the house." The liquid in her glass trembled from her shaking hands.

"There's no need to get upset." He turned to the other woman. "I really wish you hadn't brought that subject up tonight, I hardly think it's appropriate at this time."

"But what could be more appropriate than to talk about the Devil beside one of his shrines?" Evelyn laughed a thin, high-pitched laugh that pounded through Sally's head like a needle piercing her ears.

Sally was almost hysterical. "Donald, tell me *now*." She had called him by his full name and she didn't know why. Things were getting more and more confused.

"Sit down and calm down. I didn't want to tell you anything, especially after what happened the other night, but I can see now that I'm going to have to." He shot Evelyn Henderson a dirty look. "This house, as well as the Henderson house, was built by a man named Abner Sloane. He was a strange man, an eccentric who lived up here by himself. There were rumors of strange noises and strange lights from time to time, but no one really paid any attention to them until a local girl who worked for Sloane—Alison O'Keefe—disappeared. The police questioned Sloane about her disappearance, but he said he knew nothing. Several weeks later the girl's body was found in the woods near here."

Evelyn chimed in. "She had been mutilated—strange symbols had been carved on her body."

"For God's sake, Evelyn," her husband said.

"When the police found the body they went back to Sloane's house, but he was not home—or so it appeared. They broke in and found him hanging in the basement. They also found that he had been a Devil worshiper and that the basement had been converted into a temple for him and his followers. So all the stories about the noises and the lights had proved true. The murdered girl was not the first person to disappear from the area; eventually all the bodies were discovered, mutilated in the same fashion. So this was his house. So what? He's been dead for twenty years. I don't want you to start getting ideas about this place just because of its history."

Sally had listened, dumbfounded. The cellar had been his temple. It was there that the innocents had been slaughtered. It was there she had seen that figure emerging from the shadows. Was it possible...?

"Donald, you forgot to mention the most important thing. Sloane left a note pinned to his body. He declared that he would come back to the house to avenge what he felt was the injustice done to him by those who stopped his worship. The altar is still in the cellar, Sally. I've seen it myself. It looks like a pile of rocks. But those are your words, aren't they? You did say you saw the figure of whatever it was come out of the darkness by that very same altar. Isn't that peculiar?" Her eyebrows lifted and she began to laugh, the red of the lights reflected in the pupils of her eyes.

Sally closed her eyes. She wished she had never left the city.

# FOUR

Nothing Don could do made Sally feel any more sure of her safety. That Christmas Eve had been a turning point for her; she had felt it that night. The Hendersons and their ghastly stories of Devil worship and death had all but ruined the holidays for her. Even though she tried to keep up a brave front for her husband, she knew that it would be impossible for her to ever feel safe and secure in the house. She had seen something in the cellar that night, despite Don's reassurance that it had been her imagination and that there was actually nothing to fear. From that night on, Sally was on her guard.

Christmas came and went, as did New Year's Eve; each was celebrated with unusual solemnity, the holidays were not what they had been the year before. Against Sally's wishes, they spent New Year's Eve with the Hendersons. It was not that Sally minded leaving her house to visit—in fact, she was anxious to see the inside of the grotesque house where the neighbors lived—but she objected to seeing the couple at all. They had made such a lasting and bad impression on the girl that she feared even to be with them again.

But on Don's insistence they went to the house via the path which connected them. It would have been a fifteen-minute drive by way of the road, but walking, it only took five minutes. The houses were much closer than it appeared from the road. It seemed odd that a car was in this case the slowest way to get from one house to the other.

The night was bitterly cold and brilliantly clear. A full moon hung in the sky like a forgotten Christmas-tree ornament, throwing icy shafts of light into the dark, dead forest. As they walked, unseen animals moved about near them in the sparse grasses. Now and again a shadow darted across their path running toward something ... or from something unknown. It made Sally shiver to think. She was settled right in the middle of it and it seemed that it was making all attempts to recover the ground that had been stolen from it by Abner Sloane. How she hated that name. And she hated the house she had once loved.

The Hendersons were very congenial that night. There was no talk of death and mutilation, no reference made to the history of the house, no laughter at Sally's expense. There were five of them for dinner and drinks; the two couples and, of all people, Silas Dorn. How he happened to have been invited Sally was to figure out much later—and how he managed to be so nice she never did figure out. His whining condescension and obsequious behavior was displaced by a strong, very masculine personality which had not even been hinted at when Sally had first met him. It was a complete reversal. So much so that she had the distinct impression that one side of his personality was an act. Which one, she did not know.

The evening went quite smoothly. Conversation touched lightly on many subjects, all of them high-spirited. In general, the evening was a very pleasant one. But there was one thing that Sally noticed even more than she had before: she felt like a complete stranger in the group. First it had been her husband and the realtor; then Don and the Hendersons; now it was the four of them. There was an invisible bond among the four of them that excluded Sally. They were too comfortable together, the conversation flowed so easily, first names were spoken with such casualness that it almost implied years of acquaintance. Yet that was impossible. Or was it? Watching her husband that evening, Sally wondered just how much she really knew about him. All that she knew he had told her, but then that was the only way one could find out about someone—unless one hired a private investigator ... and Sally was not about to do that. It seemed so dishonest and distasteful. But there was something odd about this group, something that was probably staring her right in the face but which she was unable to see. She was silent for most of the evening, trying to decide exactly what was wrong. When she was unable to make heads or tails of the situation, she gave up and tried to enjoy herself. To her surprise, she did have a good time and it was with some regret that she left the Henderson house that night.

Walking through the woods on her way home, Sally thought of the house and just how similar it was to the one she and her husband had rented. The rooms were laid out the same way, down to the last detail. Evelyn had shown Sally the second-floor rooms. Sally had been taken aback when she realized that their bedroom was decorated identically to the Hendersons'. This fact unnerved her somewhat, for it seemed to form a bond of intimacy that Sally would just have soon done without. The rest of the decoration was Gothic grotesque. The furniture was dark-stained oak that seemed to dominate the room. Even the pictures on the walls had an ominous air about them. In fact, the whole house seemed threatening. And the disconcerting thing about it was that everything had been planned that way; it was not just an accident.

When they got home that night, cold and tired, Don suggested a fire and a nightcap; Sally couldn't have been more pleased.

"How do you like our new neighbors now?" he asked as he settled down next to her on the rug in front of the hearth. "They're not quite as unpleasant as they first seemed, are they?"

Don had been so friendly with them from the start that this question surprised her. "At least tonight we didn't talk about death and the Devil. That's a pleasant change."

He laughed. "I think I've got Evelyn and Ralph Henderson figured out. It seems to me that they want to impress us. Since we're from the city they probably feel a little bit like country bumpkins when they're with us. By talking about all that mysterious stuff to us—despite the fact that it is very unpleasant—they probably think they have an edge on us. It may make them feel less threatened."

"Well, that may be the case, but now I'm the one who feels threatened." Sally frowned lightly.

"By Evelyn? She's full of hot air, if you ask me. And Ralph is just a puppy who follows by her side ... although sometimes he shows his true colors. I wouldn't worry about either of them. Just let things ride. But remember that they are the only people for miles around, so we might as well get used to seeing them. Besides, I think that Ralph might be able to give me a few pointers about starting my business. Perhaps he could arrange a few meetings with people who might throw a little business my way. For that reason we have to at least be nice to them." He took his wife in his arms and settled back, sighing contentedly.

Sally decided that she would question Don about his relationship with the other three people. "This is going to sound strange, but I have to ask you something which has been bothering me for some time now. Ever since that first day when we came up here to look at the house, I have had the feeling that you've known these people before. Did you ever meet the Hendersons or Silas Dorn before you came to look at the house." Unfortunately her tone of voice indicated her true feeling, and the question came out almost as an accusation.

Don bristled. "What do you mean? I'd never been in this part of the state before I came to look at the house. How could I possibly know them? Besides do you think that they are the kind of people I would become friends with if it weren't absolutely necessary? You know something, Sally, you've been acting very strange lately, and I'm worried about you. First it was that business in the cellar, then it was your hysterical outburst when you found out that the house had a bad reputation, and now you're beginning to see a conspiracy around you. You've become very paranoid lately and it's unattractive." He pulled away from her and went to sit in a chair near the window.

She followed him, saying: "Don't get me wrong. It's

just that the four of you get along so well together. It's like you've known each other for years. And, after all, all I know about you is . . ." She stopped, realizing too late that she had gone too far.

"All you know about me is what I've told you. Is that what you were going to say? And do you think I've been lying to you all this time? You know, the more we stay here the less I like what's happening to us. I thought that getting away from the city might bring us even closer together, shake the cobwebs out of our relationship, but now I know that I was wrong. This house has had a bad effect on you. No, that's too easy an explanation. It's something inside you that is showing itself for the first time. Why it has chosen this particular time in our life to make its presence known, I have no idea? I do know, however, that your outbursts are becoming very trying." He tossed down the rest of his drink and stood up. "I'm going to bed now and please don't try to make anything more of it . . . I'm tired." Don brushed by her and went quickly to the staircase and up to the second floor.

Alone by the fire, Sally felt more alone than she had felt in years. What was happening to her? Why had she suddenly become distrustful of her husband after all the years she had known him. What was it about the house that made her see danger everywhere. She wondered if Don was right, if there was some flaw in her character which only now was revealing itself, forced to the surface by the solitude of her existence. On the other hand it was still possible that Don was lying to her for some reason of his own, trying to make her feel like she was in the wrong when actually . . . She chided herself for that thought and concluded that she was too confused to solve anything that evening.

Wearily, she cleaned out their glasses, checked the doors and windows, making doubly sure that the door to the cellar was fastened with the new lock Don had bought, and climbed slowly to the bedroom. When she finally slipped into bed next to her husband, she realized that he was already asleep and, for the first time in their married life, that they had not resolved an argument.

Sometime during the night Sally woke up. She didn't know why but she was suddenly awake. Had there been a noise from downstairs? She couldn't be sure. Listening with all her powers of concentration brought only the sound of the winter wind to her ears. Vaguely disturbed, she put her head back down on the pillow and tried to go to sleep. From downstairs a noise reached her. It was not the same moaning she had heard before, but something similar. Every muscle in her body tensed as she lay straining to hear it again. It stopped.

Again, not knowing where she summoned the courage from, Sally slipped to the edge of the bed and put her feet on the floor. It was cold and clammy. After a few seconds of fumbling she managed to find her slippers and slide her feet into them. Don slept soundly by her side. Should she wake him? The sound had stopped and his reaction would be the same it had been earlier in the study—disbelief.

Stealthily, the young woman slid from the bed, went to the closet and found her robe. For several minutes she stood by the closed bedroom door listening, but the house was silent. Careful not to make any unnecessary noise, Sally opened the bedroom door and walked out into the hall, shutting the door behind her. Her eyes were accustomed to the dark and she could see that everything seemed normal, in its right place. At the top of the stairs she hesitated, not quite sure whether she should go downstairs alone or rouse her husband. Imagining the cynical reaction he would have to her request for help made her decide to go on alone.

With each step she felt as if she were walking toward a confrontation which fate had decreed the minute she had seen the house. It was as if an unknown force were drawing her steadily away from the safety of her sleep into an unknown land where everyday rules had no meaning. Each step down the stairs brought her closer and closer to her destiny. She felt as if she were in a trance, being drawn quietly and quickly by some unseen force to its center. She was powerless to do anything but continue her descent to the main floor of the house. She wondered what she would find there. Would the cellar door be open? Would the voice, that strange, low moaning call her down again to meet it?

At the bottom of the stairs she hesitated. The house was silent. Even the wind outside had stopped. The only sound was her own heavy breathing which she was unable to silence, unable to control. She stood for five minutes, ten minutes with her hand on the bannister, wondering what she should do, knowing all the time that she could not return to her bed until she had satisfied herself that there was nothing—or something—in the house.

The sickly moonlight flooded the hallway where she stood, covering everything in a thin veil of translucent gauze. How odd everything seemed in this strange light. How eerie the formal living room looked. The massive pieces of furniture crouched in the corners, as if waiting to spring out at her.

She looked down the hallway toward the kitchen. It was a long tunnel of darkness that the light from the moon was unable to reach—a long, endless tube of gloom that seemed to be drawing her. Almost against her will, Sally stepped from the last step to the floor and began to walk toward the kitchen. The sound started again as she reached the doorway, but she could not make out where it came from. It could have been anywhere; in front of her, behind her, or even under her in the cellar, where it had been before. She wandered through the rooms of the ground floor, searching for the source of the noise, hoping that at last she would find it and learn for sure why it was calling to her. And she knew that she had been singled out from all the people who had ever lived in the house to become a sacrifice. She had become the chosen one and her future was no longer her own.

Sally was only vaguely aware of the time passing, of the voice calling her, of the cold of the house. For her, there was nothing except her quest. She was no longer in control of anything. Slowly, ever so slowly, she made her way through the study into the living room where she thought she heard sounds, but no one was there; no person was waiting for her.

She was about to leave the room when she noticed the chest. It was a small, ornately carved chest which she had never seen before. It had not been there earlier when she had locked the windows, nor had it been there that morning when she had cleaned. It sat on a table by the window, its lid slightly open. Through the gloom, the now-terrified girl could see a faint greenish light shining from within. She walked slowly toward it, afraid of what it might contain, yet powerless to stop herself.

With trembling fingers, she lifted the lid of the

chest and saw a large ring. The band was made of gold. It was extremely wide, as if it had been made for a man. Set in the center was an enormous emerald. It was this that gave off the greenish light, it was this which her hand went toward uncontrollably, it was this which she slipped on her finger and felt the warmth from. What did it mean? Where had the chest and the ring come from?

Sally did not know the answers, but she did know that this ring was meant for her and that the voice had awakened her and called her downstairs so she would find the ring and wear it. This too was part of the closing circle of events that had trapped her in the center, powerless to escape. Fascinated, she stared at the ring for several minutes, then rubbed it slowly against the smooth skin of her cheek. It was so warm and comforting. It made her feel so secure and safe. But why?

A sound behind her made her whirl around. Directly behind her, framed in the doorway, stood a tall figure dressed in a black cloak. A tall, pointed hood shadowed the face, and only the large, burning yellow eyes were distinct. Sally was too frightened to make a sound. The figure raised a hand and pointed a long, bony finger at her. The voice was like the moan as it said: "It is yours, and you are ours." As the words were spoken, the eyes of the creature grew in size and intensity, burning into Sally's soul.

It was only then that the strangled fear managed to wrench itself from her throat and escape as a long horrified scream.

# FIVE

When Don awoke the next morning he found that Sally was not in bed. This did not strike him as odd, however, for she had gotten into the habit of getting up before him and preparing a large breakfast. He took his time showering and dressing, as he pictured his wife in the kitchen making sausages, eggs, and toast. No rich coffee smell floated up to the second story to greet him, but still he took his time going downstairs.

"Sally," he called, when he reached the lower level. There was no answer. He went into the kitchen and discovered that she was not there. Nothing had been touched since lunch the previous day.

He left the kitchen and went into the study. The drapes were still drawn, as they had been the night before, and Sally's coat was still draped over the arm of the leather couch that flanked one wall. "Sally," he called, again looking around. It was then that Don Taylor saw his wife's body on the living room floor. At first it looked like a pile of laundry, but protruding from the bulky bundle were a pair of slipper-clad feet.

With more speed than it would have seemed possible, Don was by his wife's side. Her head was turned, all the blood seemed to have left her face. Her hair, long and silky, fanned out around her head as though it had been carefully arranged for a fashion photograph. But one would not have wanted to look at her face for very long. The young woman's eyes seemed to have sunk deep into her skull and there was a bluish tinge to the thin skin of the lids. Her cheeks, too, seemed to have sunk inward and her lips were white and taut. It appeared as if she had witnessed something that had scared her to death.

With trembling fingers, Don bent over the figure of his wife, once so pretty and healthy, now so deathlike, and took her cold wrist between his fingers. At first he could find no pulse, and he feared the worst. However, after a few minutes, he managed to locate a pulse; weak and erratic, but nevertheless there. Afraid that Sally might have broken something in her fall to the floor, Don left her where she was. He got a heavy blanket to cover her. The room was still chilly, and he wanted her to be as warm as possible.

A quick call to the Hendersons' got the name of a doctor from a nearby village. Within minutes, Don had explained what had happened and was waiting for the doctor's arrival. Evelyn Henderson said she would visit later in the day when things had calmed down.

Fifteen minutes later, Dr. Thomas Simpson arrived in a car that looked as if it had been driven out of a museum. He hurried to the door under the watchful eyes of Taylor. He was admitted before he had had the chance to ring the bell. Simpson was a good-looking man in his early thirties. His air of casual charm immediately made anyone who came in contact with him comfortable. He was just over six feet tall, with short brown hair and a carefully trimmed beard which, far from making him look older and wiser, made him look more boyish and likable. His manner was slow and relaxed with a tendency toward laughter. But despite his levity, he took his job seriously and was one of the best doctors for miles around—if not *the* best.

Even before taking off his coat, Simpson demanded, "Where is your wife?" He followed Taylor quickly into the living room. The examination took only a few minutes. Finally, the doctor said, "We should get her into bed, nothing's been broken." As they carried Sally up the stairs, the doctor asked how it had happened. When Don said that he had merely found his wife in that condition the doctor replied, "Very curious. And you didn't hear her get up during the night for something?"

"I'm a very sound sleeper. I'm afraid she could have dropped a bomb under the bed and I probably wouldn't have heard it." He paused, considering the situation for a second, then decided that it might be best to tell the doctor what had been happening over the past weeks. The young physician listened intently.

"What do you ascribe all these things to, Mr. Taylor? Do you think that your wife really saw something in the cellar that day, or do you think she was imagining it?"

"To be honest, doctor, I think Sally was imagining the whole thing. There was the story the Hendersons forced me into telling and I think that may have triggered everything."

"That may be true, but didn't you say that she saw this figure *before* she knew the history of the house. Doesn't it seem coincidental that it would appear to her before she had any reason to think that there might be something wrong with this house?" He removed the thermometer from Sally's mouth. He looked satisfied. "Normal," he said, replacing the instrument in its case. "Doesn't that strike you as a bit odd?"

Don was getting edgy. "Doctor, don't tell me that you're going to believe that story my wife told. Why, it's preposterous. It's just that she has been under a great strain these past few weeks. She's been working too hard getting the house together. You know as well as I do that solitude can sometimes play dangerous tricks with the imagination. Sally has been used to living in the city, where she could simply pick up the telephone and talk to any number of friends. We're virtually isolated here and I imagine it's taken its toll on her."

The doctor looked perplexed. "Are you trying to convince me that your wife is unstable? Has she ever shown signs of nervous exhaustion before?"

Don's voice was weary. "No, of course not. And I'm not trying to convince you of anything. I'm just looking for a rational explanation for what happened last week."

"And what about last night?"

"I have no idea what happened last night, if it did happen during the night. For all I know she may have fainted while she was on her way to make breakfast this morning."

"Is your wife subject to fainting spells?"

"No she is not and to anticipate your next question, I have no idea why she should have one now. My main concern—and I think it should be yours—is for the health of my wife. I find these questions ridiculous."

Simpson smiled, showing a set of beautifully white teeth. "And that is also my main concern. Questions bring answers and answers bring solutions. Now, if you'll excuse me, I want to wash up."

Don watched the doctor leave the room to go to the bathroom at the end of the hallway, concerned with both his wife's condition as well as what the doctor was thinking. When he returned, Don spoke up. "What *is* wrong with my wife, Doctor? We seemed to have gotten so far off the subject that I never asked."

"From what I have been able to deduce, she suffered some sort of traumatic shock which caused her to faint. Her slow pulse and other symptoms indicate that. I suspect that she left you some time during the night and something happened to her which her mind was not able to accept. When that occurs, the mind often blanks out the event and the person lapses into a comatose state purely as a self-defense. All we can do for now is to wait until she regains consciousness."

"When do you think that will be?" Don asked, his voice full of worry.

"I can't say. It may be a matter of hours or a matter of days. It just depends on how great the shock was for her and how strong her will is. I would hope that by this afternoon she will have recuperated enough to tell us what happened."

Evelyn Henderson was solicitousness itself. She appeared shortly after lunchtime and vowed that she would stay as long as she was needed, be it a day or a week. Don, too tired to argue with the strong-willed woman, let her have the run of the house. Her first job was to reassure Don that everything would be all right, that she would watch Sally until her condition changed, in which case she would notify Don right away.

So Don and Tom Simpson sat in the study before a roaring fire, each with his own thoughts about what had happened. The sun wearily made its way across the narrow winter arc of sky. The sky was ash gray punctuated by the puffs of smoke which rose from the chimney. It was a sad, moody day. In the study, where the clock was mournfully ticking away the endless minutes, the mood was grayer than the day. The two men sat opposite each other in large chairs, the doctor staring out the window, the husband watching his slippered feet make circles in front of him on the carpeting.

The clock struck three and the sound startled the doctor. He had dozed off, and now he was alone in the room and the sun was nearly gone from the sky. The room was hung with dark, heavy shadows like mourning crepe, and he cursed himself for being so unfeeling in the face of an emergency, even though the night before he had delivered a set of twins; he had had little sleep and Don's early-morning call had caught him just as he was drifting off into a really deep sleep.

The doctor was puzzled by the house and the people in it. He had lived in the area long enough to know the story of Abner Sloane and his practices. He also knew that the house had stood empty for years and had almost completely gone to seed until several months before. A host of carpenters and decorators, plumbers and electricians had invaded the small community and had transformed the house from a shambles into a showplace. Why had this happened so suddenly? Why had the unseen owner suddenly decided to spend a small fortune to have the house reconverted just to rent it out at a probable loss to some strangers from the city. It was all very odd indeed. And now this story of something in the basement and the resurrection of all the horror surrounding the house. Very strange.

Simpson's reverie was suddenly shattered by a bloodcurdling scream from the upstairs room Mrs. Taylor occupied. Don Taylor's voice floated down from upstairs filled the urgency. "Dr. Simpson, come quickly, Sally's regained consciousness."

The doctor sprang from the chair and was halfway up the stairs before he knew it. The scene that confronted him as he entered the bedroom was an alarming one. Evelyn Henderson stood in the corner of the room, her face pale and drawn, her hands pressed tightly to her mouth. Over the bed, restraining his wife, stood Don Taylor, a look of disbelief and terror spread across his handsome features. The most riveting character in the tableau was Sally Taylor herself. What had a few hours before been a waiflike, wan figure was now a fierce animal, eyes wide with unadulterated terror, lips crimson from the force of blood, and teeth savagely bared. She was forcing herself upward toward her husband, clawing at the air and trying to escape.

"Get away from me," she yelled in a tortured voice. "Don't come any closer. I've seen you before and you can't frighten me. I don't belong to you, I don't belong to anyone. Get away from me." Her last words were a scream. Then, as suddenly as it had begun, it stopped. Sally's eyes slowly rolled upward, then closed, and once again she was unconscious.

"Doctor, what in God's name happened?" Don was

trembling, almost unable to stand. Evelyn saw his plight and quickly came to his aid, supporting him and guiding him to a chair.

Doctor Simpson stood by the side of the bed, holding Sally's wrist delicately between his fingers. After a minute of studying his watch he released her, went to his case which had been set on a chair, took out a vial of clear liquid, filled a syringe and injected it into the woman's arm. "Just a sedative to make sure she rests for a while. An outburst like the last one can be very dangerous to a patient."

"What was she talking about? What was all that nonsense about not belonging to anyone?" Don tried to raise himself from the chair but Evelyn's strong fingers pushed him back down again.

Simpson said slowly, "I'd guess that she was repeating something which which happened to her before she fainted last night. She was obviously talking to someone, someone who said that she belonged to him—or her. The terror you saw was real. Her mind brought it all back and she began to reenact what occurred while you were asleep. I should hope that this might convince you, Mr. Taylor, that your wife is not just imagining things. For if she is, then she is a very disturbed young woman, though you seem to indicate that she has never had any mental problems."

"Never. Sally is the most carefree person I have ever known."

"Was the most carefree, you mean." Simpson's face was glum. "Mrs. Henderson why don't you take Mr. Taylor downstairs and make him some tea ... or a drink might be better. I'll sit here for a while. I don't think she should be left alone just yet." A thought came to the doctor as the two were leaving the room. "As a matter of fact, I think your wife should have someone around for the next few weeks to help her with things. Whatever happened to her has been a terrible shock and she is going to need companionship during the day until she is better. I know just the person for her. You think about it and we can talk later."

Half an hour later, Dr. Simpson looked up from the journal he was reading and saw that Sally Taylor had opened her eyes. He was somewhat surprised, for the drug which he had given her was very potent and he had expected that it would keep her asleep until the next morning. He dragged himself from his chair and went to the bedside. "How do you feel?" he asked softly.

Sally examined him with unabashed amazement. "Who are you?" Her eyes opened wide with fear. "What are you doing here? Where is Don?"

Simpson explained everything to her as gently as he could manage. She listened quietly, as if the words were filling blanks in her memory, then she began to cry. With little prompting, the doctor was able to get her to tell him what had happened the night before. Her voice rose and fell, trembling slightly as she related the story.

The young doctor watched her with a certain amount of nonprofessional sympathy. Whatever she had gone through had been a very real and horrible experience for her. "Is that all you remember?" he asked when she had finished.

"Yes. The last thing I saw was that figure—the same one I saw in the basement—coming toward me. It still had its hand out as if it were trying to grab me. Doctor, what is it? What is trying to get me? I know there is something in this house that wants me for its own use. I've known it from the start, and now this..." Her voice trailed off into silence.

"I don't know, but we'll find out. I promise you." He turned the lamp down and said, "Now you get some sleep and I'll be right back."

Downstairs in the living room, Simpson repeated his conversation with Sally to the two astounded listeners. As he did so, his eyes carefully examined the room for any sign of the trunk Sally had described. There was nothing that even faintly resembled it, nothing that could even be mistaken for a trunk. Had she imagined the whole thing? Or had it been there and been removed?

Telling Don to wait for five minutes before going to see his wife, Simpson went into the bedroom again to check on his patient. Asleep, the girl looked almost like a child. The terror and strain had been replaced by a calm, tranquil look produced by the effects of the drug.

A thought suddenly occurred to the young man. With one swift motion he pulled Sally's hands from under the coverlet. There on her finger, as she had said it would be, was the heavy gold ring with the green stone affixed in the middle.

Simpson realized that Sally was in terrible danger. Without saying a word to anyone, he slipped the ring from her finger and put it in his pocket, already trying to decide what his next move would be.

# SIX

Don entered the room cautiously a few minutes later. Disappointment at not finding his wife awake showed on his handsome features, but he managed a smile when he saw that Sally was sleeping peacefully. He stood at the edge of the bed, staring down at her. "She's been through so much these past days and I still don't understand what's happened." His eyes asked for an explanation from the doctor.

"I think she's been through more than we can really know," Simpson said gravely. "It will be up to you from now on, Mr. Taylor, to see that your wife is never left alone. In fact, I think it might be a good idea if you both left this house altogether."

Don looked astounded. "Can you be serious? We've just moved here. You can't really believe the stories that Sally is telling. Why, it's incredible. People in the cellar, people in the living room, men in cloaks. I can't take it seriously."

"But you know the history of this house? You know what it has stood for for years?"

"Of course I know that, but everyone connected with it is dead now. This is just a house, it's not human—or inhuman. I think that Sally has imagined everything that she has told you, and it worries me."

"It should. You must realize that even if there is nothing happening here, even if it is all in her mind, the fact still exists that she believes it—believes it so much that she is frightened to the point of nervous collapse. You must take her away from here or there is no telling what the consequences will be." Simpson took out a pipe and packed it carefully, not bothering to light it. "Bad for the health," he pointed out. "And remember, there is no concrete evidence that what she says happened did or did not happen. We have no way of proving that anything *did* happen. And that being the case, I think it would be wise of you to take her away from the scene of all this recent unhappiness."

Don looked puzzled. "I don't know what to make of it. You said she sounded so sure about that chest and the ring, yet I couldn't find any trace of a chest downstairs."

"And the ring?" Simpson queried.

"I hadn't thought of that. Let's look." He gently lifted the covers from his wife and examined her hands, his eyes narrowing as he did so. "Nothing," he barely whispered, his eyes catching those of the doctor.

"Mr. Taylor, you almost sounded as if you expected there to be a ring."

"No, of course I didn't. Well, maybe I did. If there were a ring or a chest, then I could reassure myself that Sally was in good health mentally. Not finding one makes me wonder about her sanity."

The doctor picked up his bag and began putting

his instruments back into their proper places. "There is only one thing you can do if you want to keep your wife and that is to get her out of here, take her back to the city . . . anywhere. In the meantime I will send Mrs. Chambers over tomorrow to look after her. I think it would be a good idea if you prepared a room for her—at least for a week or so. She's a trained nurse and she'll be able to handle any situation that may arise. I will visit tomorrow night and will try to drop in as often as possible." He left the room, still conscious of the weight of the ring at the bottom of his coat pocket.

The next day dawned with the clear brilliance characteristic of certain midwinter days. The unseasonal heat melted the delicate casings of ice on the trees, and everything for as far as the eye could see shimmered with moisture, like tiny jewels scattered during the night.

Sally awoke feeling slightly dizzy and light-headed. She had no clear recollection of what had happened to her, nor did she realize that she had missed an entire day. The room was full of sunlight, and was surprisingly cheerful for that time of year. Her first shock was to realize that Don was not beside her, and from the looks of the bed, he had not spent the night with her at all. Her second shock was to realize that it was nearly noon. She had never, in all her life, slept that late; it seemed so wasteful.

When she tried to raise herself out of bed, she realized that she was too weak to even move her legs from under the covers. Panic gripped her. What had happened? Her mind frantically sought the answer. As she lay there, deep in thought, the events which had forced her illness came rushing back to her and with them the emotions were rekindled. For several minutes she lay in the bed too terrified to even try to move. But it was daylight and she was safe and that was a comfort. In a voice that was almost too weak to recognize as her own, she called out for her husband.

A minute later the door opened and someone stepped in. It was not her husband, but a stout woman well into late middle age. The woman made no noise as she entered the room. In fact she appeared to float, so effortless were her movements. Sally got her first good look at her as she moved past the windows toward the bed.

She looked to be in her early fifties, certainly no older, and her grandmotherly manner seemed to support that estimate. Her hair was nearly all gray. It was pulled back severely from her face and twisted into a bun at the back. But instead of making her seem cold and spinsterish, the hairdo made her more motherly and added an air of warmth and friendliness which Sally felt immediately. She was reminded of an aunt she had, an unmarried woman whose understanding of children and young adults could disgrace the most proficient psychologist. This comfortable association helped to form an immediate bond, silent though it was, between the two women. Her dress was simple, practical and unadorned—no need for frivolities in her case. All in all, this woman seemed to be a plain, no-nonsense type, a country woman who could proudly trace her stock back for generations.

Seeing that Sally was awake, she stood at the foot of the bed and said: "I was beginning to wonder if you'd ever wake up. They tell me you've been asleep for thirty-six hours." Her voice was slightly teasing, yet understanding at the same time. "I'm Mrs. Chambers. Doctor Simpson thought it might be a good idea for me to keep an eye on you for a few days. You've had a nasty shock."

Sally stared in disbelief. What was this woman saying? Asleep for thirty-six hours. Dr. Simpson. It was all too much for her. "I'm afraid that I really don't follow you, Mrs. Chambers. Where is my husband? I'd like to talk with him." Her voice was reedy and plaintive, like a child calling for help.

"Mr. Taylor had to go into town for a little while. He'll be right back. Now, is there anything that I can get you? You must be starving." Her eyes twinkled. "I've just made some fresh bread and soup from the leftover chicken I found in the refrigerator. Can I interest you in that? You look as if you need something to put a little color back into your cheeks."

Sally was about to summarily turn her down when she realized that she was enormously hungry. If it were true that she had slept for such a long time, then she obviously hadn't eaten. The thought of fresh, hot bread and homemade soup made her think twice before she answered. "That sounds like the best offer I've had," she paused and continued rather sadly, "in days. What happened to me? You must understand that I can't remember anything."

Mrs. Chambers took her hand and patted it gently. "Your husband will explain everything when he gets back. But, right now I want you just to lie back and relax; don't think of anything. You're all right now and nothing is going to hurt you." She left the room in a flurry. Mrs. Chambers had obviously made herself at home.

Fifteen minutes later the door opened and Mrs. Chambers entered, carrying a tray with several dishes on it. After setting it aside and propping Sally up in bed, making her as comfortable as possible, she retrieved the food and placed the tray on the young woman's lap. "This should be a good start on the road back to health. If my chicken soup doesn't cure you of your troubles, you might as well give up." Her voice was jesting, but there was a serious undercurrent to what she said.

It was plain that cooking was one of Mrs. Chambers' strong points, and when Sally tasted the first bit of soup and the crunchy crust of the still-warm bread she had to allow that it was the best she had ever had. Halfway through her food, she said, "Why didn't my husband go to work today? His vacation has ended."

Mrs. Chambers looked amazed. "And leave you in the condition you're in? He's been worried to death about you. The only reason he went to town at all was to get enough food so that you wouldn't have to worry about it when he does go back to work. I don't think I've ever seen a man so worried about anything in my life. He's as nervous as a cat ... but I can't say that I blame him." She looked reflective. "I never thought I'd see the day when I stepped back into this house, not on your life."

Sally finished her small meal and let the older woman take the tray from her. "Why wouldn't you ever want to come back to this house, Mrs. Chambers?" She wanted to sound naive enough to elicit the full truth from the woman. Mrs. Chambers apparently enjoyed talking, and Sally was hoping that she would be able to get her into a conversation that would fill out the gaps Don's story had left.

Mrs. Chambers waited a minute, pretending to arrange the few things on the tray to her satisfaction. Then she said, "I thought you knew about this house.

Why, everybody in these parts does. I don't see how you could have missed a story like that."

"You forget that we're from the city. We're just renting the house and there is very little that I know about it, except for something which my husband once said about the former owner. You must also realize that if there is anything we should know it is your duty to tell us, especially since we have a five-year lease on the place."

"I suppose you're right, but I'm not sure that now is the right time to tell the story. It might upset you after what's happened to you ... although it might also help to explain a few things."

Sally felt a cold shiver race up her spine. What could the story of the house possibly have to do with her two encounters unless, of course, what Abner Sloane had threatened to do had come true. Didn't Evelyn Henderson say that he had promised to come back to avenge his own death? It seemed like nonsense. Sally was about to shake the whole idea off as insane when she remembered the sight of the figure the previous night, coming toward her with outstretched arm, demanding that she go with him, declaring that she was his ...

Mrs. Chamber's voice droned on through her thoughts, until she heard her say, "If you think you're up to a rather gruesome story then I'll tell it to you. But, mind you, don't let your husband know that I told you. He wouldn't appreciate it."

"I won't breathe a word of it to him," Sally said, a little excitedly. Suddenly she felt like a little girl again, sick in bed with her favorite aunt about to tell her a story to make her feel better. Only this time the story was not bound to make her feel better, though it might help in the long run—like the pain of a novocain injection to deaden the more serious pain of a tooth extraction.

Mrs. Chambers drew up a chair and pulled it close to the bed. In the bright sunlight her gray hair shone silver, and from where Sally lay it looked like a metallic corona surrounding the shadowed surface of the woman's face. She cleared her throat several times and began. Her voice was well-modulated, her matter riveting, her skill as a storyteller undeniable.

"This house was built about thirty years ago by a man named Abner Sloane—that much you know. The house which the Hendersons live in was also built by Sloane, but about ten years before this one. At the time no one could figure out why he wanted two almost identical houses. Of course it was all explained later when everything came out.

"Now, without giving away my own age, let us just say that I was a child when the first house was built—not a babe in arms, mind you, but still young enough to have that part of my life clouded by a faulty memory. So what I know of that period I've heard from my family and other people who were living here at the time. I suppose they're just as reliable as I am. And that means that we're all subject to human frailty and error, so what I've got to tell may have been embroidered a bit—although I'd say that most of it is straightforward.

"Sloane, it seems, appeared out of nowhere one day with a lot of money and a pretty young wife. When I say 'out of nowhere' I simply mean that he and his wife were not from this area and no one had ever seen him before he arrived in town that day. In those days—and I can remember this myself—the town was smaller than it is now, if you can believe that. There were two or three stores, the church of course, and the houses you see now, but not much else. The depression somehow hadn't managed to affect our lives, although we were very much aware of its existence. Several of my father's friends had left to go to the cities, and it was during that period that they all returned home, never to leave again.

"Sloane had a brand-new car which he and his wife used to drive around in all the time. They were like visiting royalty when they first appeared. I guess it was the car which initially set them apart from everyone else, made them look suspicious. You can imagine that people in a town as small as this one stick together like honey to a comb. And it was true. From the minute they arrived, they were something special. And when we learned that they intended to stay here, to build a house, it was the most remarkable thing which had happened in years." The woman adjusted herself in her chair and yawned slightly. "Not as young as I used to be," she muttered, and rubbed her eyes in a very lazy manner and continued with her story.

"Now I don't want you to get the impression that they were grand or anything of that sort ... not in the least. They dressed like anybody else and talked like people from the country. It was just the car that set them apart. It was a monstrous thing, all black with shiny chrome here and there and enough room in its back seat to fit five people. No one around here had ever seen anything like it, and I pray to God that we never do again.

"Anyway, they spent several days looking around the countryside for a suitable location for a house and settled on the land where we are. All in all, Sloane bought well over a hundred acres for himself and his wife. When the deal was settled, he brought in his own team of carpenters and electricians and got the house going. The rumor was that he even hired an architect from the city to do the plans. At any rate, this infuriated the people in the town. Our own men would have been more than willing to do the work for him, but he chose to go elsewhere. You have to realize how this affected the people in the town. It was as though this man—this stranger—had decided to snub everyone. It was a mistake on his part and their reaction, in the long run, was a mistake too.

"The town made him an outcast before he had even moved in. Not a soul would have anything to do with him or his wife. He never indicated that it bothered him, but his poor wife had to bear the brunt of the dishonor. Everytime she came into town to buy something, people treated her as if she were dirt. They refused to talk to her. When she even said hello she was snubbed. One day it was too much for her and she broke down in the general store and became hysterical. Sloane had to be called. When he arrived, they said it was like the Devil himself had ridden into town. He took his wife into that car without saying one word to anyone, but it was obvious that there was hate in his heart. Mrs. Sloane never went back to town again. In fact, she was never seen again by anyone.

"After this event had happened people began to feel a little guilty, so they sent someone out to the house a week or so later to act as their spokesman and inquire into the health of the poor woman. Sloane met the man and, before he had a chance to apologize, he cursed both him and the town and said he hoped that nothing but evil would come to it. So fierce were his oaths that the man rushed home and was unable to tell what had happened until the following day." Mrs. Chambers looked up at Sally. "I'm not boring you, am I?" she asked, knowing full well that the young woman was spellbound.

"Of course you're not. I find it fascinating." Sally readjusted herself on the pillow and asked the woman to go.

"Now that I think about Mrs. Sloane's breakdown in the store, I think that maybe it was not the town's silence which did it to her. It was probably what she was going through with her husband in that cursed house. But at that time no one had any idea what was going on, and had they been told they never would have believed it.

"It was about this time, after the incident with Mrs. Sloane, that local farm animals, began to die mysteriously. At first it was thought that the occurrences were isolated, but a definite pattern had set in. Death came suddenly, as if a plague were moving from house to house, touching each member of the village. There were cattle found dead, horribly disfigured— not from an animal or man—but as if something evil, something deadly, had gotten inside them and killed them by destroying their insides. They would be found in the fields, tongues stretched out, eyes bulging and heads twisted into grotesque positions. The veterinarian from a nearby town was called in, but all he could say was that they had suffocated. There were no marks on their bodies and no chemicals in their blood. The whole town was in an uproar, not so much because of the loss—it was usually only one animal to a family—but because of the fear which these deaths brought, for no one could determine how they had died. And fear of the unknown is perhaps the strongest fear of all.

"It was about that time—which was now several

years after Sloane had made his first appearance—
that Hattie Clark went insane. Hattie was my age, and
she was from one of the town's best families. It was
Halloween and we had all dressed up in costumes to
go and gather candy—kids haven't changed in generations. After we had gone around in the town, it was
Hattie who decided we should walk out to the Sloane
place and spy on them, maybe even give them a good
scare. She wasn't a malicious girl, it just seemed like
fun at the time, so we all agreed. It's a long walk
from town and by the time we got there, we were too
scared to do anything but turn around and go home.
But not Hattie. She said she had gone there to see
them and she was going to.

We waited for her on the main road while she went
to the house by herself. I can still see her figure walking up that dark path through the woods to this day.
It seemed like ages had passed and there was still no
sign of our friend. We were about to go after her
when we saw her walking back toward us. Her face
was white as chalk and there were tears streaming
down her face. Her hair was tangled and dirty, with
little bits of twigs caught in it as if she had run
through the woods. When we asked her what had
happened she didn't say a word. She just passed by
us and began walking into town. We followed her,
not knowing what else to do. It was as if she were in
another world all by herself. She knew where she was
going but she was oblivious to everything around her.
By the time we reached the town she had started
screaming. I have never in my life heard a sound as
terrified as that scream, and I hope that I never do
again. The doctor was called that night, but there was
nothing he could do. Nothing he gave her had any effect on the poor thing. The next day, I heard many

years later, she began to shout the most blasphemous obscenities at everyone. She cursed everyone and everything and couldn't be stopped. For the next few days you could walk through the town and in the silence hear her voice raised to a feverish pitch, uncontrollable and inhuman.

"Finally a doctor from another city was called in and he declared that the girl had gone insane. She was taken away and put into a state institution where she died about ten years ago. The shock of everything was too much for her parents, and her mother, who was then only in her early thirties, got sick and died. Several days later, her father killed himself. To this day, no one has any idea what happened to her. But, needless to say, it gave people the excuse to go after Sloane who had, by this time, become an object of fear and hatred.

"Because there was nothing that could be done legally, a group of men from the village went up to the house one night with the idea that they would lynch him. It was foolish, of course, but such was their anger. When they got to the house, Sloane came out onto the porch and said that if anyone tried to harm him or his wife he would kill them. He didn't have a weapon with him but there was something about the way he spoke which scared the men to the point where they fled the house and never returned. That would have been the end of it had it not been for Alison O'Keefe." Mrs. Chambers got up from her chair and said, "I've parched my throat doing all this talking. I'm going to get some tea, would you like a cup?" Sally nodded yes and the woman picked up the tray and left the room.

Sally took the opportunity of Mrs. Chamber's absence to think about what she had heard. So far there was nothing but circumstantial evidence to link the man Sloane to anything that had happened in the town. As far as she could tell, there was nothing to indicate that he had anything to do with the cattle dying, and there had been no direct involvement with the little girl. It seemed to be one of those cases where people had needed a scapegoat to blame and Sloane had been chosen because he had slighted them—probably unintentionally. Nevertheless, it was a horrible story. The idea of a poor child going insane and dying in a madhouse was in itself horrendous. If it was connected with the man who had built the house she was now in, then that was even more terrible.

Mrs. Chambers returned with tea and cookies. "The tea will revive your body, and my cookies will revive your spirits. I may as well tell you that I have a reputation of being the best cook for miles around, although you would certainly have discovered that by yourself." There was a mischievous twinkle in her eye. She poured two cups, passed napkins and sweets, and asked seriously, "This story isn't upsetting you, is it? I'd hate to have your husband after me for bothering you unnecessarily."

Between bites Sally said, smiling, "On the contrary, I find it fascinating. A little sordid, perhaps, but still fascinating." She thought for a second. "Tell me, Mrs. Chambers, what do you make of this story. You've lived with it for years. Do you see any connection?"

She smiled slyly. "I've got my own ideas about this house, but you're going to have to make up your own mind. Besides, I haven't finished yet." She broke off a bit of cookie and continued. "Years went by after that particular incident. The town settled down and the matter was all but forgotten. The Sloanes were never seen again and nothing was ever heard of them except from the girls who braved rumor to go out there to work. It seems that there were now children, but they were kept by themselves.. Not even the girls who worked there saw them, although they could hear them. It was at this time that the second house was built. At the time, no one could figure it out, now of course we know it was where he practiced his worship, or whatever you call it. He lived down there where those people live," she said rather distastefully, "and he worked here, in this house."

"During the years before Alison O'Keefe came to work here, there were several cases of people disappearing, though at the time it was never connected with Sloan. I guess the village just wanted to forget that he existed at all. The people who vanished were not a real part of the town. They were men working around at odd jobs, or people just passing through. The townspeople always considered that they had just up and left without saying good-bye. I suppose, had it been someone that everyone knew, there might have been some suspicion about what was happening. But no one really paid any attention.

"Anyway, the point of the whole story is Alison O'Keefe. She was the daughter of a widow who lived near the village and made her living by doing laundry and some sewing, things of that nature. From the time she was old enough Alison was at work. Her mother was getting on in years and needed all the help she could get. There was nothing else in life for the young girl, so she went out early every morning, spent the day cleaning someone's house, and came back late every night. It was backbreaking work but it was the only thing she knew how to do and she did seem suited to it.

"I'm not sure how she got the job at the Sloane place, but she did. I think the only reason she took it was because it paid so well, even though it was a daily job. She had worked at it for nearly a year when she disappeared. During that time she never revealed anything about what went on at the house, unlike the two or three other women who had worked there. In fact, she was the only one who ever stayed much longer than a month. The other women came away frightened to death. They told stories of strange noises and sounds coming from all over the place, of how odd Mrs. Sloane was always walking around in a dressing gown as if she were in a fog, of how the voices of the children who were never seen chanted strange songs over and over again.

"She knew what she was getting into when she took the job. She had heard all the rumors about Sloane, all the tales about the strange goings on, the lights, the noises, the figures in the wood at night. But as I said, she needed the money. The odd thing was that she was never allowed into *this* house. The only place she ever worked in was the Henderson place. But Alison was not the type of girl who asked questions, so she was content to do what she was told and take her money home every week to her mother.

"Then one night she didn't come home. Mrs. O'Keefe was in a panic. She called the police, who told her to wait. When the girl still hadn't returned the next day, they went out to investigate. Sloane said the girl had left the house at her usual time and that he had no idea where she might be. He pointed out to the police that the roads were dark and dangerous and that she might have had an accident on her way home. A thorough search of the surrounding countryside showed nothing. The police gave up their search until someone in the town told them about the reputation Sloane had. This time they went back to the house armed with a search warrant and turned the place upside down. But they still found nothing. They neglected one fact, however, and that was that there were two houses belonging to Sloane. They never looked here.

"Some weeks later a man from the village was out hunting when he saw Sloane walking through the woods carrying something large in a burlap sack. The man followed him, being careful not to be seen, and watched Sloane as he dug a hole—what looked like a grave—and dumped the sack in. After he had left, the man uncovered the hole and opened the sack. Inside was the body of Alison O'Keefe. She had been brutally murdered.

"The police came immediately to this house. Sloane must have seen them, for he went to the basement and hanged himself, leaving a note that he would return to avenge his death. At any rate, the police made a complete search of the house and found Sloane's diaries which detailed his worship of the Devil and the sacrifices he made. He had started with animals and eventually worked his way up to humans. Alison was the fifth such victim. But he made the mistake of using someone from the village, someone who was known by everyone. Actually, she had ventured to this house by herself one day and had caught him in the middle of one of his rites. He had no choice but to kill her. The police also discovered that his wife was dead and that the children were gone. To this day no one knows what happened to them—if they existed at all. The bodies of the other victims were found scattered around the woods in the locations indicated by the diary. All of the victims had been mutilated and disfigured in the same fashion as Alison, carved with the horns of the Devil. It was too horrible.

"At any rate, the Hendersons came along many years later and bought the house where they live and now you're here in this house. I'm just sorry that all this has had to happen to you, although I don't believe for a minute that Abner Sloane has come back as he said he would."

A female voice from the doorway broke into Mrs. Chamber's monologue. It was Mrs. Henderson, Evelyn, and she had obviously been listening. "And just what do you believe, Mrs. Chambers?" Her voice was acid.

Mrs. Chambers was ruffled, her voice like ice. "I haven't had time to decide, Mrs. Henderson. I'll be sure to let you know when I have." She abruptly stood up and gathered the tea things before leaving the room. "In any case, Mrs. Taylor I would be careful if I were you. You never know whom you can trust. Good-bye, Mrs. Henderson."

The older woman's meaning did not escape Sally. There was a distinct animosity between the two women that was as thick as heavy cream. But why? Sally liked Mrs. Chambers and could put up with Evelyn Henderson, although she was not the warmest person she had ever met.

"Old busybody," Evelyn said angrily. Then she smiled. "I hope she hasn't been filling your head with a lot of rubbish. You need your rest right now more than anything. She wouldn't be here if the doctor hadn't insisted." Evelyn acted as though something had been spoiled.

"Frankly, I'm glad she is. The way I feel today I

couldn't do anything for myself. I'm sure that she'll be a great help when Don goes back to work."

"By the way, where is Donald? I expected him to be home." Her eyebrows raised in a peculiar fashion that was all her own.

She sounds very demanding, Sally thought. "He'll be right back, just went into town to do some shopping."

"Good. Well, I'm going to rush off now. I just wanted to see how you are. And you look much better than the last time I saw you. Now take care of yourself and don't put too much faith in what Mrs. Chambers says. She's been around these parts since Methuselah and I think it's affected her brain."

Sally was getting a little angry at the way this woman was treating her. "If you remember, Evelyn, it was you who started this whole business on Christmas Eve. If it hadn't been for you, I probably wouldn't have heard anything about it, so don't be so quick to condemn."

Anger flared across the woman's face, but just as quickly as it appeared it disappeared. "Right you are. I'd forgotten. Well, in any case, I wouldn't be too affected by what you hear. These woods are full of stories. I really do have to be going. Now take care of yourself and I'll be back later to see how you're doing."

Don't hurry, Sally thought to herself. Since they had moved in, this woman whom she really didn't like, had become a too-important part of her life—at Don's insistence. He was always saying that they should get to be friends. Well, she knew that could never happen, but if it made him feel happy, they would see the Hendersons whenever he wanted to.

Evelyn stopped by the door. "I almost forgot. I found this out in the hallway and I didn't want you to lose it. It's very pretty, where did you get it?" She extended her hand and out rolled a thick gold ring with a brilliant green stone set in the center. "If it's too big for you—which it seems to be since it slipped off your finger—I'd suggest you wear it around your neck on a chain. Well, see you later." She left in a hurry.

Sally sat for several minutes staring at the ring, feeling the fear mount within her. It was *the* ring. The same ring she had seen in the chest. And now she knew that it had all been real. And she knew that whoever had come after her that night would not stop until he succeeded in making her his sacrifice.

# SEVEN

It took Sally only two days in bed to recover from her experience. During those days Mrs. Chambers was in constant attendance and Evelyn Henderson spent much time with her. Sally was sorry that she had flared up at the woman, but it was understandable considering the strain she had been under. Both women recognized this and the incident was not mentioned again. Dr. Simpson returned and Sally became acquainted with him for the first time.

The one person who did not seem able to fall into the regular routine of the house was Don. From the moment he returned to find his wife awake and on the road to recovery his whole attitude seemed to change. It was obvious that he was worried about Sally's health, and he did everything he could to try to make her comfortable. But over and above that there was something else. Something that appeared to be bothering him all the time. When questioned about it, he merely said that there were problems at the office and that things would straighten out in time. But Sally doubted this.

Don had never been the type of man to bring the problems of the office home with him. In fact, he made it a habit never to even discuss his work with his wife. Now, to suddenly use that as an excuse made the young woman feel that he was holding something back, and she was sure that that something had to do with her. Several times she caught him staring at her with wonder. It was not a pleasant feeling for he seemed to be appraising her, trying to decide what was going on in her mind, what she was thinking and feeling. Without ever directly questioning her about what had happened the night she had received her shock he apparently was trying to decide for himself what had really happened.

That was the problem. What had *really* happened that night in the living room?

Sally had gone over the events so many times that she wearied at the thought of them. She knew, deep inside herself, that she had not imagined the man, or the chest. It *had* happened and the ring she now wore around her neck was the proof of that. But for some reason she had not told Don about Evelyn giving her the ring; she kept it a secret from him. And she did this to see what his reaction would be. Did he think that she had lost her mind that night and imagined everything, or did he really believe her? Either situation was a cause for worry and the strain of it was beginning to show in their relationship.

Never before had the two of them fought. Yet in the past few days they were at each other constantly, arguing over the smallest things, things which would have had no importance if their lives had not become so confused. At every opportunity Don would question Sally's judgment, her actions, her desires. He had become so much of a tyrant with her that she had chosen to move her things into one of the other bedrooms. They were going through the first real crisis in their marriage, and she was afraid.

For the next few months the subject of the history of the house and Sally's experiences were forgotten—or at least not mentioned. The couple had decided individually that it would be best that way. They returned to the routine of daily living and they never spoke of the matter again.

But that did not mean that Sally did not think about it. She was convinced that she was in danger, that whoever had come after her that night was not about to give up. It was just a matter of time, as far as she was concerned, before something happened again. She only hoped that when it happened she was not alone. Mrs. Chambers had been kept on, against Don's wishes, to help around the house. After all, it was an enormous place, with more rooms than Sally had ever tried to manage before. It seemed that she had just finished dusting one room when the next was dirty, and by the time she had finished that one the first was in need of another cleaning again.

She and Mrs. Chambers spent most of their time straightening the house, cleaning and talking. Talking was the older woman's specialty, aside from her cooking. Indeed, it was probably the cooking that soothed Don's nerves when he arrived home every day from the city. In the months since she had been with them Don had gained fifteen pounds. He was not too happy about it, but he enjoyed the food so he never said anything.

The snow and ice of the winter gradually disappeared until one day, upon getting up, Sally discovered that there had actually been a thick blanket of green hidden under the white. There wasn't a trace of snow to be seen anywhere, even on the mountaintop in the distance. The air, too, seemed to have been cleaned of the close, cold feeling of winter. The scent of rich, warm earth filled the house, and in the distance the sounds of returning birds cheered the day. It was the beginning of everything new, the end of the dead season. It was spring.

From that first warm day the mood in the house changed. Everything seemed a joy, every little job and chore. Even Don didn't mind the long commute into the city as much as he had during the dark days of winter. Sally was glad now to have the opportunity to get out into the warm sunshine and see about starting a garden. It was the thing she had looked forward to during the winter months of confinement. There had never been a chance to grow things in New York, nothing could survive in that air. But now she would grow flowers and vegetables and in the summer they would have fresh things from the garden and during the next winter they would eat what she had put up herself. She had to laugh when she speculated about canning things. It was so unlike her. Yet wasn't her whole way of life now so unlike anything she had ever done before?

The thought of growing things prompted her to think about starting a family. If she were to get pregnant now, during the next winter she would be raising her first child. They would sit by the fire together and she would sing to him—she still counted on a boy—and during the day he could keep her company. The whole idea was so wonderful that she could hardly contain herself, she was so happy.

During these spring days Dr. Simpson kept regular attendance at the house. What had started off as a purely professional routine had become something very nice and personal. Sally got along famously with him; it was as if they had known each other for years. Don was rather reticent. He seemed to object to the attention paid to his wife by the doctor. On the other hand, he never said anything, nor did he ever make his feelings known, even though Sally suspected he was jealous and found it rather funny. There was no one else in the world for her except Don, nor would there ever be.

One day the doctor dropped in just before Don got home. He explained that he was just passing by and thought he would stop in. But it appeared that he was there for another reason. After a while he said, "Sally, do you remember the ring that you said you found? The gold one with the green stone? Well, I've got something to tell you. I took it. I was the one who took it off your finger. I hope you're not angry, I had my reasons."

Sally sat quietly for a second, not knowing quite what he was talking about. "But that's impossible." she sputtered.

The doctor's eyes opened wide. "What do you mean? I have it right here in my pocket." He reached his hand inside his coat and produced the ring.

Sally stared at it as if it were alive. "But how do you explain this, then?" she asked, as she slipped the ring on its gold chain from underneath her blouse.

They stared at each other silently. At long last, the doctor carefully removed the ring from her neck and examined it closely. Then he compared it to the one he held in his hand. "They're identical. Where did you get this one?"

"Evelyn Henderson gave it to me the first day I was awake. She said she found it in the hall and suggested that I wear it around my neck so I wouldn't lose it again. Where did you get that one?" The fear she had managed to repress during the past months began to slowly fill her veins.

"I took this one off your finger the day after your encounter. I wanted to have it examined. I sent it to a friend of mine in Seattle who is not only a damned fine physician, but an expert on the occult. He returned it yesterday. And you said that Evelyn Henderson gave it to you? You can see that they're identical. I wonder where this one came from?" he questioned, tossing the heavy piece of jewelry around in his hand. "Have you told Don about this?"

Sally blushed, for it seemed that she had been caught deceiving her husband. "Well, no," she stammered trying to think of a suitable explanation for her actions. "I didn't want to upset him. He's been so happy in this house, I knew that if he saw the ring he would want us to move out and I don't want that." As she was saying this she wondered if it was really the truth.

"And you're willing to take a chance with your life so that Don can have a nice house? What will it be like if he's alone here?" Simpson seemed angry.

"What do you mean alone here. I'm not going anywhere." The words were silly, because she knew what he was about to say.

"There is something that both you and your husband should know and I think that now is the right time to hear it. Sally, you are in great danger. You didn't imagine anyone attacking you that night, someone actually did. And the person you saw in the cellar was also there. Someone wants to kill you."

If he had drawn a gun, Sally couldn't have been more surprised by the impact of his words. Suddenly she felt alien, in an evil house; nothing seemed to belong to her, nothing seemed familiar. The room spun slowly round and round and she could hear the sound of heavy breathing; it was her own. She felt as though she was going to faint. "I don't believe it," she managed to gasp. "Who would want to kill me? You can't be serious."

Simpson got her a glass of water. "I've never been more serious in my life. Every minute you spend in this house is just another minute you bring yourself closer to harm. I would have thought you could have seen that. I was sure Don knew that you were in trouble."

"Don thinks I imagined the whole thing. Sometimes I'm not sure myself."

"But don't you see that that's the idea. You had two encounters with this person within, how long? Days? Weeks? The second time you had a severe shock. Nothing happened, but maybe the time wasn't right. Then nothing. Now you have let your guard down again. You say you're not sure that anything happened, and that's exactly what someone wants ... to keep you in doubt. Don't you see that you're being toyed with? It's an evil, dangerous game and you're the prize. What do I have to do to make you believe me?" He leaned forward and took her arm, the strain showing in his face. "You and Don have to get out of here before something else happens. And if it does, I'm afraid that it will be more serious than you can imagine." He relaxed now and leaned back in his chair, exhausted from the surge of emotion.

Sally was confused. She always thought that she had not seen the end of the terror, but now to have it put to her so forcefully unnerved her. Her immediate reaction was to pick up her things and flee, but she knew that would do no good—there was Don to consider. She had to talk to him, tell him her fears, and make him see that they had only one way out. But she needed to know more. "What did your friend say about the ring?" she managed to ask.

The doctor looked grim. "He said that the ring belonged to a cult of Devil worshippers and that its symbol—you can see horns faintly engraved on the stone—is the sign of the Devil. I imagine that Abner Sloane belonged to this cult and that these are, or were, his rings. If that is the case then there must still be someone around here who still practices his rites. And that person, or persons, wants you for its sacrifice."

"Isn't there anything we can do to stop them?"

"Of course there is. We could call in the police and have them arrested. But first we have to know just who is doing this to you. There's got to be an explanation." He thought for a minute. "You said that Evelyn Henderson gave you this second ring. How did that come about?"

"It was the day I first started to feel well. She was here for a short visit and she said she had found it in the hallway. I figured it was the same ring I had found in the chest."

"Didn't it strike you as odd that she would give you the ring and not comment on the fact that it matched the description of the one you had seen the night before? At the very least it confirmed your story. I wonder why she did that ... unless she knew it was not the same ring, but one which she supplied herself."

Sally didn't like the thought. Despite the other woman's rough manners and occasional hostility, she was a friend of Sally's—the only one, in fact—and they saw each other almost daily. The idea that Evelyn could be involved in a plot as sinister as this was hard to accept. "I can't believe that Evelyn would want to harm me," Sally said.

"It's not so much that she wants to harm *you* as it is that you are a means to an end, a sacrifice to their god. She has nothing against you personally, all she wants is your life."

"My life?" Sally asked rather hysterically. "Is that all? I thought it might be something important."

Simpson saw that Sally was getting overwrought. "Calm down. We have no proof yet, nothing concrete to go on. It's all supposition. I could be so far off the mark that what I'm saying is nonsense. But the important thing about this is that until you—we—know who's behind this, we have to suspect everyone. And given the fact that you know very few people here that rather narrows it down, doesn't it?"

"No. It's just possible that there is another person—or persons, as you put it—who figures in all this. Why must it be someone from the inside? We are all alone out here, isolated from everything around us. Anyone who wanted to get into the house to do whatever they wanted would have little trouble. It is just possible that the second ring was planted on the stairs where someone would find it. That person just happened to be Evelyn. It could have been Mrs. Chambers or Don or even you. I don't like the idea that the people I love and trust are working against me."

"Of course you don't, and maybe they're not. But maybe they are. That's the point. You're going to have to be on your guard from now on, time is running short."

"How do you know? If everything is so much a mystery, why can you be so sure about this?"

Simpson sighed and looked hopelessly into the girl's eyes. "Because I checked the records and very shortly it will be the twentieth anniversary of Sloane's death. What better time to sacrifice someone than on his death day?"

# EIGHT

When Don returned home, having missed the doctor by minutes, he found Sally in a very depressed mood. Her discussion with Simpson had made her feel alone and vulnerable. She felt as if she could trust no one at a time when it was so very important that she trust everyone. Her world was closing in on her and a fate over which she had no control had taken the strings of her life and was manipulating them like a marionette master.

"I've asked the Hendersons for dinner tonight. I know it's late but I saw Ralph in the village and he mentioned how long it's been since we last saw them. I bought some extra food so Mrs. Chambers can cook something special." For the first time he saw the look on her face. "What's the matter with you? You look as if your best friend just died."

At the sound of that word Sally broke into tears and raced into the arms of her husband. "Don, I want to leave this house. I want to get out. Something is wrong here, something is waiting for me. I can feel it." She looked at him with imploring eyes, tears running down her silky cheeks.

The pressure on his arms from the grip of her tightly clenched fists was actually hurting him. "What's the matter? You've been good all these months. Why do you suddenly want to leave."

"What do you mean I've been good? You act as if I've been a naughty child. Don't you realize that someone is trying to kill me? Isn't that obvious to you." She found it hard to believe that her husband could be so callous about this situation. She was desperately afraid and he was acting as though she was crazy. Maybe that was it. Maybe all these months he had put up with her because he thought there was something wrong with her mind.

Don pushed her away. "It was Simpson, wasn't it? I knew he would be trouble from the start. What has he been telling you?" There was a cold cruelty in his eyes that she had never seen before. "Well, tell me." He stood, waiting for an answer.

"He thinks we should leave this house. He thinks it's dangerous for me to stay here."

"And you take his word over mine—your husband. Do you think that if for one minute I thought you were in danger I would allow you to stay here? What do you think I am, some kind of monster? Sally, I always thought I knew you, but now I'm not so sure. Ever since we moved into this house there has been nothing but trouble. If I let my imagination wander I'd say that this might just be your way of getting us back to the city. If it is, then I don't like it at all. It's dishonest. If you want to leave then we'll leave but that is the only reason, let's not go on pretending that you're in danger." He stalked from the room.

Sally felt her whole world crumbling around her.

nothing made any sense any more. Her husband either thought she was a liar or a crazy woman. And an acquaintance, practically a stranger, believed her. What was she to do? She was so full of indecision that when Mrs. Chambers asked what Sally wanted for dinner she only shook her head in dismay and told the woman to ask her husband.

The Hendersons arrived in high spirits at seven, their usual time. Evelyn looked ravishing in a dress she had bought on one of her infrequent visits to the city. The countrified air about her was gone and had been replaced by a very studied and perfect sophistication. Even Ralph looked different. He was dressed in a dark suit with a rep tie rather than the hunter's outfit that he usually wore, and he looked like a Wall Street Broker. Their manner and dress lent an air of celebration to the house, although there was no reason for it. In a way it was good that they had dressed like that, for Don and Sally had not spoken since the scene earlier. Sally was more hurt than angry, but Don, on the other hand, was overtly hostile. She had never seen him like that and it worried her. Nothing had worked out from the day they moved here, and she knew that when they left they would be two changed people.

"You look very pretty," Sally said to Evelyn. "Is that a new dress?" Conversation—make conversation in order to forget.

"It sure is. I got so tired of my flour-sack dresses that I went to the city and went wild. I even managed to get Ralph to come with me. He's no longer the best-dressed man voted by *Field and Stream*." She laughed her deep-throated, grating laugh, throwing her head back at the same time. Sally only smiled.

Seeing this, the woman said, "What's the matter with you two? Looks like you've had a fight. Anything I can do?"

Sally was about to decline politely when Don interrupted and suddenly, without warning, told the other couple everything that had happened. It was like having their most secret moments together thrown out for public scrutiny. As he spoke his voice was edged with anger and contempt. He glanced repeatedly at his wife out of the corner of his eyes. Sally sat dumbfounded, not knowing what to make of the situation and beginning to feel more and more foolish with every passing minute.

The Hendersons listened quietly and seriously. When Don had finished, Evelyn said, "Donald I think you're being a little too hard on Sally. You know there are two distinct possibilities. One is that something happened; the other is that it was imagined. In either case, it seems understandable to me that Sally is upset. For whether it did or did not happen, Sally went through a bad experience and it's only natural that she should want to get away. I know if something like that happened to me, I'd be in such a state of nerves I'd have to be sent away for good."

"I agree with Evelyn," Ralph said. "Maybe what you need is to get away from here for a while. A change of scenery, as they say. Let your mind rest." He smiled like a kindly grandfather.

Sally had had enough of this kind of talk. Ever since she had been frightened, people had treated her as if she were an eccentric. Now, after fuming for months, her anger flared.

"You all sit there and talk about me as if I were crazy. Well, let me tell you, I'm not. If you don't believe me, there is one person who does." She sat back defiantly.

Evelyn smiled cautiously. "Who is that, dear?"

"Dr. Simpson. He believes that I am in danger. Besides if I had just imagined meeting that thing in the living room, how do you explain this?" And with that, she pulled the ring out from under her blouse. There was silence from everyone present.

"Why that's the ring I found in the hallway, on the stairs. Is it something special?" Evelyn asked, leaning forward a bit to see it more clearly.

"It's the ring I found in the chest that night." She paused. "No, no it's not. The ring I found in the chest was taken from me by Dr. Simpson. He's had it examined by a friend of his. This is a second ring, a duplicate."

Now the silence in the room was heavy, oppressive. The Hendersons sat huddled next to each other, their faces blank, their eyes narrowed. Don's face was a mask of surprise. "You've had that ring all along, and you never said anything about it to me? Why?"

Sally looked rather ashamed. "I guess it was a test. I wanted to see if you believed me, trusted in me. I didn't show you the concrete proof because it was very important to me that you took what I said seriously. And now I guess I know the answer to that question." She lowered her head sadly.

"That wasn't very fair, Sally," Evelyn said. "Didn't it ever occur to you that Donald didn't want to believe it because he didn't want to think that you were in danger? That was a very cruel thing to do." She stared at the girl with a new interest, as if seeing her for the first time.

Donald got out of his chair and went to his wife's side. "I'm sorry I ever doubted you, but Evelyn is right. I can't bear the thought that you are in danger, that something might happen to you." He toyed with the ring around her neck. "And I guess this is the proof that something is going on." He smiled at her.

"I shouldn't have done it, Don, but I've been so unsure of everything since we moved here. I guess I was just desperate. But now that you know we can leave, can't we? We can get out of this house and get as far away as we can? Please!" The tears started again.

"Of course, dear. As soon as possible. I'll arrange everything." He kissed her lightly on the head.

The Hendersons watched the couple in silence, tight, drawn smiles distorting their features.

The next few weeks Sally was in heaven, for she and Don had finally decided to move away from the Sloane house. The decision had been arrived at the very same night the Hendersons had dinner with them, the night Sally had revealed the ring around her neck. Don was taking time during his lunch breaks to look for an apartment for them back in the city. But this time it would not be the small bachelor-type apartment they had shared after their marriage. It would be something larger, something which could accommodate themselves and their family. For Sally was now seriously thinking of starting the family they had always talked about. She needed a purpose to her life, a goal which would give it new meaning; and children seemed to be the answer.

Those weeks she spent getting ready to leave flew by. There was not that much to do, considering that the house had been furnished, yet she was able to occupy her time getting her clothes and other articles in order. Now housework was a joy and the house even seemed to be a happy place. Sally constantly found herself whistling and talking blithely to herself. She had told Mrs. Chambers that they were moving and that she would not be needed any more. The older woman had seemed relieved that her friends were getting away from the house.

It was only the Hendersons who seemed offended. For some reason they took the news as a personal affront, as if it were because of them that the young couple was leaving. Sally mentioned this to Don. He hadn't really noticed it before, but he was quick to agree with his wife. He supposed that since they were the only people around whom the Hendersons had any contact with, they were probably more hurt than offended. He suggested that when they were all together, that Sally should not sound quite as happy as she did about the move.

She hardly had the opportunity to practice this restraint, for the Hendersons seemed to have disappeared—at least for the time being. Whether it was because of something private which kept them away, or merely their feelings about their friends' departure, the fact was that they had not called or dropped in for some time. Sally noticed this with some curiosity, but her own excitement and concern for her new life left her little time to worry about the other couple.

It was a week before they were going to move back into the city and it was such a beautiful day. Sally had spent the morning out in the garden wistfully thinking that she would have to give up all her plans to grow flowers and vegetables. It had sounded like a good idea at the time, and she still fancied herself an amateur gardener. But the idea of leaving the house was so overwhelmingly attractive that she soon put the thoughts in the back of her mind and decided that canned food would be good enough for her.

Don had left for work at his usual time that morning, telling her before he got in the car that he had found an apartment in the city which would be perfect for them. Sally was so overjoyed that she burned the eggs and toast, and scalded the coffee. Don had known about the apartment for weeks, but he had wanted it to be a surprise. That very day he was going to sign the lease for three years, and they would be able to move in immediately. It was going to be a wonderful day.

After lunch Sally had nothing to do; the packing was done, except for things they had to use until they moved. There was no shopping to do (besides Don had taken the car to the city). The Hendersons were not in touch, so there would be no company—it was a day of peace and quiet, a day to sit down and read and be happy. After several hours of *Moby Dick*, Sally got restless. The sun was beginning its long ride to the edge of the horizon. As it moved the air became more and more chilly. It had been a warm, sunny day and Sally had even chosen to open the windows wide in the study and sit in front of them, feeling the new air lazily caress her soft skin. Now the windows were closed and the young woman was sporting a cardigan sweater to fend off the cold.

She wandered aimlessly about the house. The joy and excitement of the move had worn off, leaving her with an empty, unsatisfied feeling. She had known this sensation before.

For some reason Sally went upstairs. She looked through the various rooms as though she had never seen them before. They were nice rooms, newly decorated. Not one of them showed any signs of what they had once been used for—if, in fact, they had been part of Sloane's "workrooms." For the first time since she had known she was leaving, Sally thought she might miss the house, for the structure itself was very pleasant and inviting. It was just the history and the associations which unnerved her ... and, of course, what she had seen and experienced.

On her way back downstairs she noticed a door which she could not remember having seen before. It was set against one wall, near the top of the stairs, and seemed to have been designed for a child, it was so small. She tried the knob and discovered that it was unlocked. With the spirit of a fearless adventurer, she opened the door and peered into the darkness. A long, narrow flight of stairs rose away from her into the attic. At the top, a dirty window let in the last of the daylight. For a moment she hesitated on the threshold. Then, never thinking of any possible danger, she found the light switch, flicked it on and began to climb upward.

The attic was so laden with dust that Sally immediately began to cough and choke. It was obvious that no one had been up in this room for many years. Once she reached the top of the stairs she could see why. The room was large, covering the entire top of the building in one vast expanse. No abutments or chimneys interfered with the space. It might have been converted into another entire set of rooms had it not been for the fact that the ceiling was so low in places that a person, even if lying down, could not have fitted. Even at its highest point, the ceiling was just taller than Sally by a few inches. Any living done in this room would have had to be done sitting down.

There were several windows around the attic, but

all of them so dirty that barely any sunlight was able to penetrate. With the exception of the dust, the room was empty, or so it seemed at first. Sally was about to return to the main floor when something caught her eye in a corner. Because of the scanty illumination from the lightbulb, she had almost overlooked it. But now, she was anxious to discover what it was. Carefully stepping over some rotten floorboards Sally made her way to the corner and examined the object.

After a few seconds she realized that this trunk, this chest of drawers, was the same one which she had seen in the living room the night she had been attacked. With trembling fingers she pulled open each drawer and peered inside. There was nothing. It was empty. But she did notice that on each drawer, on the flanges of the pull-handle, there was a small engraving of what looked like a horseshoe with pointed ends. She stared at the markings, wondering where she had seen them before, for the symbol was familiar. Then it suddenly dawned on the girl that these were the same signs that were on the rings she had been given: they were the signs of the Devil.

Sally took her hands off the chest as if it were the most vile thing she had ever touched. The sign of the Devil; the accursed horns of Satan. Just the thought of them made her flesh crawl with disgust. She remembered that she still had the ring around her neck; she had never bothered to remove it even after Dr. Simpson told her what it meant. Quickly she unbuttoned the top buttons of her blouse and removed the thin gold chain from around her neck. The ring hung heavily from its support, its green stone glinting viciously in the half-light. A feeling of intense hatred welled up in the young woman and, with one powerful throw, she hurled the ornaments across the room into the dust.

As the ring hit the floor with a resounding crash, Sally felt something at her neck, as if something unseen was touching her, making its anger at her gesture known. So real was the feeling that she let out a scream and turned about, expecting to see something standing behind her. There was nothing. Nothing but the memory of those cold hands on her throat ... if they were hands.

The experience was too real and too frightening. She could not stay in the attic any longer. She ran toward the stairwell as fast as she could, being careful to keep her head low. As she came within touching distance of the bannister, her foot caught in a loose floorboard and she tumbled forward, scraping her knees on the rough surface of the floor. For a moment she lay still, the pain though slight, still throbbing. Sally carefully massaged her twisted ankle and ran her hand along it to feel for broken bones. There was nothing. Shaking from fright and pain, she got to her feet and was about to leave when she saw that she had dislodged a plank in the floor. Something underneath caught her eye. There was something hidden under the floor.

With little effort Sally managed to remove the contents of the secret cache. In the dimness she could make out a sheaf of crumpled papers, crudely written on in pencil. What they were or how long they had been there she could not tell until she saw them in the light. Before going downstairs she quickly flipped through them, noting the same childlike handwriting all the way through. On the last page there was a signature which she could not quite make out.

Taking the papers closer to the light she read in horror, the name crudely scrawled on the last page: Alison O'Keefe.

# NINE

Clutching the tattered pages in her hand, Sally went back downstairs to the study. She pulled up the same chair she had sat in so quietly minutes before, turned on the lights and the radio, and tried to read calmly. It didn't take long before that calm was destroyed. The written words sped by as if they had a life of their own. Nothing Sally could do would stop or slow down the speed with which she read. She was, for the minute, possessed by the spirit of the girl dead twenty years. She was reading so fast that she realized that in her excitement she hadn't understood the meaning of the words. Pulling herself together, she began again.

I am a prisoner in this house of the Devil. I have been kept in this attic room for the past week without any more food than a cup of soup or some scraps from their table which the dogs turned down. Each night he looks in on me and brings the food. Sometimes it is the oldest child, the girl with the vacant, cruel eyes who brings it. She is worse than her father, for he at least ignores me. She treats me like an animal, like something she would not want to touch, and all the time she enjoys the pain which I feel, the humiliation, the degradation. I sometimes feel that the children are the really evil ones, not Sloane and his wife. But in the end it will not matter, for I will be dead, as they will, and God will judge us all.

If I had known that the stories about this man were true I would never have come to this house. But who believes in stories of ghosts and witches, other than children? I have never been afraid on Halloween once I was past the age of eight, and I have never feared anything I could not see. Perhaps it is the teachings of the village priest that have made me not fear what other people do, for if I am to think this life is just a middle ground for my soul, then what happens here to me matters little. I am trying to convince myself that these words are true, that they are the only things which are important to me right now, but that is not so. I am afraid. I am more afraid for myself and those around me than I have ever been in my life, for I have seen the Devil at work, I have seen his slaves practice their rites and I know that for this I must die. I am so afraid.

Sally noticed that the writing stopped almost at the bottom of the page and when it took up again it was more relaxed and more uniform. Alison O'Keefe must have left off writing for one reason or another then picked it up again at a later date.

... I started work for the Sloanes because my mother was sick and could not support us any longer. Of course I had heard all the rumors about what went on in their house. I also knew that once they had been very badly handled by the people of the village, whose consciences were probably not clear yet. People can be so vicious when they have been caught in the wrong; unforgiving to the last.

So it was with this attitude that I accepted the job with them. And the pay was better than I could have found elsewhere. I talked to Maggie Taylor, who had worked for them for two weeks, and I asked her if there was anything I should know about before I went. She said that my life would be in danger and that I must be out of my mind to even consider the job. When I asked her what she meant, she merely smiled and said nothing. I think she was just trying to get attention, for whenever the subject of the Sloanes's house came up she would smile dramatically but say nothing. I think she probably had been caught stealing there, just as she had at Madeline Davis's, and would not admit she had been fired. So she was no help. Besides, I always wondered about the girl's mind—if she had one.

I took the job and was happy there for quite a while. The house itself is very strange and peculiar; even more so inside than it was outside. But once I got used to it, it seemed like any other house. Mrs. Sloane was a very nice, gentle woman, who seemed to have had a great deal of sadness in her life. She was always lying down in the sunroom, with her head propped on a silk pillow and that small, strange dog of theirs resting at her feet. Once or twice I came into the room and she was crying to herself. When she saw me she turned her head away so that I couldn't see the tears, but they were there anyway. She seemed to get more and more frail each day, until finally a few weeks ago she died. I was sorry to see her go, for she was really the only one in the house who treated me civilly. No one knew she was dead and Mr. Sloane asked me not to tell anyone. I respected his wishes.

Mr. Sloane, himself, seemed to be a nice gentleman, although he was subject to fits of temper which almost brought the house down. There was one time that he caught me when I went into that tower room where he was always studying. All I wanted to do was to clean it, for I had never even seen it in all the time I worked there. He came at me with his fists clenched. He threatened to beat me within an inch of my life if he ever caught me in there again. But normally he was good to me, though he used to walk around the house in a daze, his eyes closed, bumping into furniture and knocking things over. I decided that he was sick—one way or another—and that was why he had such a reputation with the people in the town who thought him odd. How wrong I was.

Mr. and Mrs. Sloane seemed like nice people, although each was decidedly odd. I was wrong; I know that now. But then the stories and whisperings seemed like a fantasy. Who would have ever believed them all? And it is the children who are the real monsters.

I have always liked children, and I even hoped

to have some of my own. I know now that that is impossible; I will never live that long. But as God is my judge, I have never seen children such as these. There are three of them—a girl and two boys. They vary in age from twelve to six; the girl is the oldest. She looks like her mother and acts like her father. Yet there is something else about her. Another influence which I cannot figure out. It is something so strange that on occasion I have seen the old man cower away from her as if she held some special power. What can it be?

She acts more like an adult than a child of twelve. I have never seen her smile, and I doubt if she ever does. For her, the world is a place of sadness and cruelty. What could have happened to make her like that? What inhuman force has taken over her soul? For if anyone were one of the devil's own, it is this large, awkward girl with a sweet face and dead eyes. She is the one who taunts and teases me. It was always like that. I would clean and five minutes later there would be a pile of dirt she had brought in from the outside. Her mother just watched through the veil of her sadness; her father was nowhere to be found. What could I do? I was paid to do work, not train children. But now it is different. It is she who comes to see me, who sticks me with pins and calls me names so vile I dare not even think about them. And all the while her father lets her do this to me. Why?

The handwriting had again degenerated into a scrawl as if the girl knew that her time was limited and she was writing as fast as she possibly could. The last few words were blurred. Sally could imagine this poor, frightened girl huddled in the attic of the house, crying her eyes out, knowing she was going to die but not knowing when.

Sally looked around the room cautiously; it felt as if there were someone watching her. All day long she had had that feeling. On several occasions she had become so uncomfortable that she had moved to another room. But now she ascribed the sensation to this small diary written by the doomed girl so many years before. She turned back to the pages.

The other children, the boys, seem to be under their sister's power. It is not as if she bullies them, or treats them badly. It is just something unspoken, an understanding between them that she has power over them—whatever that power may be. The boys have been nice to me, in their own ways. For the most part they ignore me—for which I am grateful—and while I was working they even tried to be of some help now and again. They never visit me here in this attic. Perhaps they do not even know that I am here.

I am imprisoned now because I stayed late one night and I saw too much. God forgive me for being curious, but there is nothing I can do about it. I cooked supper one night—which was unusual, because Mr. Sloane usually did it—and stayed to clean up the dishes. It was about a week ago—I've lost track of time in this dark room—and even though it is now spring, it still gets dark rather early. When I left the house it was dark. There had only been the boys and Mr. Sloane at dinner; the girl was not to be seen. As I left I looked up toward this house where I am now prisoner, and saw lights. I would not have thought anything of it, except that the light was not coming from within the house, but from somewhere outside. It looked like someone had started a bonfire. I thought that it might even have been a forest fire. I hurried up to the house, and it was then that I saw that horrible sight which I will never forget—even after I am dead. Dancing around the fire, stark naked, were Mr. Sloane, his daughter and sons, several people I have never seen before and one person from the village whom I knew all too well. I had been running at such a pace that I stumbled right up to them because I was unable to stop.

When they saw me they all stood still. I will never forget that moment. There was nothing to be heard but the whistling of the wind through the trees and the crackling of the fire. Then there came a sound that chilled my heart. The sound which came from one of them was like a moaning, a low animal moan. It grew louder and louder, until I had to put my hands over my ears to stop it. I couldn't move. Something kept me there, kept me hearing that sound and watching those faces full of hate. The sound grew louder and louder and I heard my voice being called by one of them. They began to move toward me, their arms outstretched, calling my name. I felt faint but knew I wasn't going to faint. Nothing would save me from that horror. When they were finally around me, I slumped to the ground and begged their mercy. They laughed.

That night they had been calling for a sign to indicate the sacrifice to their god—the Devil. It is almost time for what they call the "rites of spring." They were all happy to see me, they could not have been more overjoyed. They had a human sacrifice to offer—me—instead of an animal, which is the highest tribute they can pay. Someone struck me on the head and when I awoke I was here, in this attic. And it is from here that they will take me to a place where I will be sacrificed to the Devil himself. God protect me!"

The music in the background was soft and sweet, gently caressing. For Sally it just punctuated the sadness of the words she was reading. The short diary of the doomed girl was so restrained, so pitiful, that tears formed in the young woman's eyes and slowly rolled down her cheeks. She felt as if she were there in the attic twenty years ago, tormented by that evil family, carefully writing down her story for someone to read and understand, trying desperately not to think of the fate that waited for her. What a terrible thing it must have been to sit and wait with nothing to do but wonder what death would be like and how it would be done.

Sally lay the papers down in her lap and tried to control herself. It had all taken place years ago. She had nothing to fear from them, they were all gone ... or were they? Someone had tried to get her. Someone who had decided that she would be the next victim. But who? Her mind raced back over the girl's words. She had seen someone from the village whom she recognized at the ceremony which had sealed her doom. Who could it have been? Was her—or she—still there? Was this the person who had confronted Sally? Again the feeling she was being watched came over her and she looked around. Nothing but the fading sun in the study. No figures, no cloaks and hoods, no rings. Nothing.

She picked up the remaining page and read.

They will be coming for me shortly. I have had nothing to eat or drink for a day. Maybe that is the way they prepare a victim for sacrifice. What will they do to me out there? How will I be killed? I pray to God that it is quick and merciful, yet at the same time I know that it cannot be; it would be too human of them.

The girl has been up here many times today. She is in a state of ecstasy. I cannot bear to watch her when she is near me, it is so obscene. I wish that I never had been born, that I had died as a child in my mother's arms. What can she be thinking now? Now that I am gone from her. It must be difficult. She could never really understand the world or the people that lived in it. Perhaps she is better off. At least her ignorance protects her and her priest comforts her. What have I but a few more hours to live in torture?

It is just possible that no one will ever find these words I have written. I don't know where I will put them. If they find these sheets of paper they will destroy them, for they fear justice and law despite their claims to be all-powerful. If I had not found the writing material in the old trunk, I think that I would have long ago gone out of my mind, the tension and degradation have been so intense. Someone is coming.

Whoever finds this, please remember me and remember that all I ask is that these people, and people like them, be found and stopped for my sake—for all our sakes.

Alison O'Keefe

Sally was trembling. It was one thing to hear the story of murder and quite another to read the victim's own words and thoughts. The line "Someone is coming" must have meant that her death was near, she was about to be taken from the house to the woods to be sacrificed, to be slaughtered like an animal on the altar of Satan. A wave of terror swept over Sally. The altar of Satan. But there was an altar in the basement of the house. She had even seen it, seen that figure emerge from the shadows near it. Could it be . . . ? Was it possible that Alison had been murdered in the basement of the house she now sat in?

The thought was too horrible. She tried to remember the story Evelyn Henderson had forced Don to tell that night. How had it gone? Alison had disappeared and it wasn't until someone from the village saw old man Sloane carrying something in a sack through the woods that her death was discovered. If he was carrying her, then it was quite possible that she had been killed in the house and removed to the forest later. Sally fought back a wave of nausea. Why hadn't Don told her? Why had he taken this house when he knew its history, its horrible, perverted, gory history?

Carefully, despite her agitation, Sally folded the papers and put them in the desk in an envelope of things she wanted to take with her. She would tell Don about them when he got home. She would confront him with this new story and ask him all the questions that had been plaguing her. Suddenly she thought of her husband and the way he had been acting lately; erratic, irascible, not at all himself. Then he would change and become loving and kind. Why the swing from one to the other? What was wrong with him? Sally decided that she would not mention anything until she was back in the city, away from the house, and near her friends, just in case ... just in case, what? Was she afraid of her own husband? The thought worried her.

Returning to the chair, Sally tried to concentrate on the music, to let its flowing melody tranquilize her troubled soul; but it was no use. She was alone in the house with the memories of the tormented words of the dead girl. And the fact that she now realized that she was sitting above the blasphemous altar where murder had been committed did little to ease her mind. All the relief she had experienced because of moving vanished and was replaced by a mounting fear for her own life. She was unprotected, alone. If something happened who could she turn to?

Finally, unable to contain her fears, Sally went to the telephone and dialed Don's office number. She would ask him to leave a little early to be with her. There was no need to explain why, for she was still uncertain of his feelings about her fears. The phone rang several times before it was finally answered.

"May I speak with Donald Taylor, please." Sally's voice, unused for the entire day, sounded strange to her ears; weak, timid, hesitant.

An officious voice at the other end said: "One minute, I'll ring his secretary." There was a long pause during which Sally could hear the ghosts of other conversations coming over the wires. "Mr. Taylor's office, may I help you?" This voice belonged to Marjorie Winston, Don's secretary.

"Marjorie, this is Sally Taylor, is my husband there?"

There was a slight pause, then the other woman said in a voice tinged with surprise, "Mrs. Taylor, your husband hasn't been in all day. He called this morning about ten to say he wouldn't be here." Her tone seemed to require an explanation.

Sally was stunned. Where could he be? Why hadn't he told her that he wasn't going to the office? But this was not the time to speculate. Gathering all her strength, and trying to sound as though everything were under control, Sally said: "Of course, I'm sorry. I completely forgot. He told me a week ago that he had an appointment about a new apartment. I'll see him when he gets home. Thank you, Marjorie."

"You're quite welcome, Mrs. Taylor," the other woman said with a snide inflection.

Damn her, thought Sally. But the feeling passed quickly, for she was too worried about Don's whereabouts and her own safety to think about the bitchiness of a secretary. She put the receiver down in its cradle and thought about what to do next. There were the Hendersons. She would call them. Evelyn would be only too glad to have a reason to visit. She seemed to view Sally as a curiosity, a strange woman whose flights of fancy and overactive imagination led her into the most improbable situations.

She let the phone ring ten times. No answer. The only person left to call was Dr. Simpson. A minute later she was talking with his answering service. She was informed that the doctor was out of town and would not be back until the following day. The following day—what could happen to her by then? There didn't seem to be any real reason to feel threatened, yet that was the way she felt.

She had to get out of the house, run from its ugliness and terror. Without thinking, she put on her heavy coat and ran out into the yard, intending to get into the car and drive into town where she would wait until Don returned. Once outside, she realized with a shock that Don had taken the car with him to work ... or wherever he had gone, He took the car only in emergencies, but today he had taken it anyway. She was stranded.

Standing in the yard with the setting sun drawing a veil of black over the landscape, Sally realized how isolated she was. It had never occurred to her before because she had always had someone around. There was nothing to be seen for miles around but the forest, the forest with its masses of gnarled, twisted trees in the foreground and its fresh, new trees in the distance. The wind blew mournfully through Sally's hair, whipping it roughly against her face. It seemed all the forces of nature and chance had decided to act against her. She was at their mercy, unable to act against them, unable to protect herself.

Sally turned to go back inside, but stopped. The house stood silhouetted against the sky like a malignant growth. She had never really noticed its shape against the darkened sky before. Now, seeing it this way for the first time, she was glad that she hadn't. It was a stark building, angular and harsh, with corners that looked jagged in the dim light. The steep, pointed roof clawed its way heavenward, seeming to reach toward something unknown. The light shining through the front door made the front of the building look like an enormous face with a gaping mouth that drew the girl forward into its innards. For some reason, fear perhaps, she didn't want to return. But she could hardly stay out in the cold and the dark. At least inside she could see what she was up against. Outside she faced the unknown on its own ground.

In a few quick, short steps she bolted into the house. As she locked the front door Sally managed to see that lights were shining in the Henderson house. Without even consciously thinking, Sally ran to the telephone in the hallway and dialed the Henderson number again. This time she let it ring fifteen times. Still no answer. Tears of anger and frustration coursed down her cheeks. If there were lights there had to be people. Why didn't they answer? She thought of going down there but reconsidered. If they weren't home and had just left the lights on in order to keep intruders away, then to return to her house she would have to walk through the woods over the long heavily camouflaged path.

Without even taking off her coat, Sally threw herself in the chair in the study and huddled thinking. The radio played on. An announcer broke in to mention the date and to say that a special broadcast was being played that night in honor of Igor Stravinsky. It was "The Rites of Spring!"

Fear gripped Sally with such a hold that she thought she would suffocate. The rites of spring. Twenty years since Alison O'Keefe was murdered! Twenty years since Abner Sloane had threatened to return . . . and she was alone.

Sally had no idea how long she sat in the chair. The music poured forth from the radio filling the room with the crashing sounds of pagan rites, screeching Devils, and terrified victims. She was powerless to stop the noise. Something inside her kept her anchored to the chair as if it were her last bastion of sanity. For Sally knew that tonight she would be alone. Tonight she would have to face the culmination of the evil plans which had been worked on her for the last few months.

It was as if she had been placed on the top of a slide the first day she had moved in—the first time she had even seen the house—and with each passing day she had begun to descend further and further, faster and faster, toward a fate which she could only guess at. It was this feeling of helplessness, this feeling of being in the hands of someone else—someone unknown—which made her angry; for she was angry with herself for not having acted sooner, not having enlisted someone's help to stop the tide of events.

Sally felt that it was almost ludicrous that she should now be sitting in that chair in that particular room, knowing that somewhere outside, perhaps even inside, the forces of evil were gathering to come and take her. If she had only acted before this would never have happened. But *if* is a big word—and meaningless—under the circumstances.

From somewhere deep inside herself, Sally summoned up a kind of courage. She could not be sure if that was exactly what she should call it, for she had always thought of herself as a timid person. But in this case she was dealing with her own life, not the lives of others—although she felt at that moment that if she were ever to be called on for assistance she could rally and do anything to alleviate the anguish and fear which she felt, and knew others also could feel. This rush of adrenaline lifted her from the chair to her feet.

Once she was standing, she acted quickly. Praying that the agents who were converging on her were still outside the house, she went through every room, turning on lights and locking windows and doors. Something from her childhood came back to her as she scurried from room to room, the actions were so familiar. To escape the city she and her family had always taken a house on the ocean during the hot summer months. One year, when she had been nine or ten, a hurricane had swirled from the southern waters up the Eastern seaboard. For days she and her family had waited for its arrival, tense with fear, yet unwilling to leave the house and return to what they knew would be safety. It was odd that they chose to remain, but typical of the stubborn streak which ran through all of them.

Finally the day arrived. The clouds grew black and the rain was so fierce that it seemed able to penetrate the wooden siding of the house. She and her parents had gone from room to room as she was now doing, locking windows and sealing all the doors in an effort to protect themselves. The storm had passed and little damage had been done to the house. They were glad they had stayed to weather out the storm, for they would have felt like quitters if they had left.

Perhaps this was the reason that Sally had been reluctant to leave this house, even though she knew that there was danger. On the other hand she had decided to leave, to run away. And now it was too late. The decision had been taken from her. She was alone with no one to help her, to guide her. And strangely, Sally felt somewhat exhilarated by the idea. Not that the prospect of death stimulated her; but its nearness provided her with the will to go on, to triumph over it.

She finished locking up the house, careful that she had closed everything possible—even the attic windows. She was sealed in. Sealed into a tomb of her own making. Nervous, and suddenly tired, she returned to the study and sat down, throwing her coat onto a chair opposite her. The music on the radio had changed. It was Mozart. The precise delicate sounds were exactly the opposite of the mood she felt.

One thing confused and worried her. Where was her husband? She had felt like a fool making up that lame excuse for his secretary when it was obvious to both of them that he had taken off without letting her know. What could have been his motive? No matter how she tried to think of a reason, she was unable to come up with an answer. Unconsciously, she sat waiting to hear the sounds of the car grinding up the gravel drive to the house. It was such a usual occurrence that she convinced herself it would happen at any minute. Yet, when there was nothing, when she knew that he would not be there, she was not surprised. It was like waiting for a letter in the mail and convincing herself it would be there when she got home, but all the time knowing that it would not. There was a certain comfort in the expectation, even if the actual event would not occur.

Sally sat in the chair for a long time, not knowing what she should do, not knowing if there was anything she could do. Outside, the wind picked up and began its own symphony of noises. She could hear it making its way through the young, green leaves, tearing them and scattering them before they had the chance to grow. It whirled through the strange trees around the house and whistled through the twisted, gray branches.

The wind mirrored the girl's emotions; rising and falling, strong, then weak, never the same. There was bound to be a storm—still another thing which would force her to remain in the house waiting. She eagerly listened for sounds, for something that would announce the arrival of her confrontation. How would it begin? With the moaning she had heard before? With the sounds of footsteps in one of the rooms she had thought she had secured? With the scream of a dead girl from the basement? Or maybe Sally would have to be the one to set things in motion.

Everything was set up. It was like the workings of a fine clock; everything was in place, every wheel had its purpose, every cog touched the one next to it. Waiting. Waiting until something gave it energy, something touched the pendulum and started it moving the wheels, moving the cogs, starting the machine working. Was Sally the force that would start the mechanism of her own fate? Could this thing she waited for be so cruel as to make her the instrument of her own death? She sat in the chair thinking these things, a fierce headache growing, the room spinning slightly before her.

A thin sob escaped from her throat. She had no control, no desire to try to stop it. It was the one thing which showed how she felt inside, the one release she had from the tremendous tensions she was under. Her throat quivered, uncontrollably shutting off her air supply for a second. Panicking, Sally stood up and felt the blood pounding in her head. Everything was beginning to get hazy, her eyes throbbed, her neck ached. She was not going to faint, she knew that. Fainting would be an escape and for her there would be no escape.

Outside, the rain began to fall. At first it fell slowly, like an extension of the wind, rustling the few leaves on the ground and turning over small pebbles. It grew in strength, making a sound like footsteps circling the house then merging into a rush of noise which sounded like a thousand drums resonating louder and louder. The wind shifted and the rain slashed across the windows—like pebbles tossed by malicious children. The insistent, pulsating sound followed wherever she went. It was the kind of sound which could make anyone expect to see some malignant, rainsoaked face pressed against the window.

For this reason, Sally sat back down and shut her eyes. "Don," she called out, realizing that it was useless. "Where are you? Why aren't you here?" She waited for an answer, knowing that it would not come. But just saying his name, made her feel good and momentarily safe. She heard someone talking—a woman with a frail, frightened voice. It came from within the room where she sat, very near her. What was she saying? She listened closely, riveted to her seat. "If you were only here, then everything would be all right. We could share this together. You could take me in your arms and convince me that everything will turn out. You could reassure me that we will always be together, even when everything else has fallen apart. You could take some of this terrible fear away from me. Oh, why aren't you here?"

The voice faded away to almost a whimper, a slight sob choking it off. Sally sat listening for several minutes, waiting for the voice to return. Then she realized that it had been her own voice she had heard. She had listened to herself as if she were someone on the outside. Was she really that simpering woman she had heard? Surely she must be stronger than that. Surely.

She would call Dr. Simpson again and if he was still out, then she would call the Hendersons. The answering service said he would return the following day. There was the possibility that they could be wrong. If she couldn't reach anyone she would call the town. There was a small taxi service which some of the commuters used to take them to the station each morning and drive them home each night. She would call it, have a cab pick her up and drive her to ... where? There was no hotel in the village. She had no friends, and she doubted if the driver would take her all the way into the city—at that hour the trains had stopped running into the city; they only brought weary workers home from it. Besides, she didn't have the money for a trip of that length.

Molly's Inn. Why hadn't she thought of it before? It was an ideal spot, the place where she and Don had eaten that first day she came up with him. Sally remembered that there were rooms for rent upstairs. Probably charming rooms done in early American style, with fourposter beds, lace, china basins, pitchers and beamed ceilings. It would be ideal. Sally's feverish mind fastened on each detail of the inn with a tenacity that only the obsessed have. She knew that thinking about the warmth and comfort and security of the inn made her feel good, made her feel as if danger were the last thing in her life she had to worry about. She felt a warm rush of tenderness for the inn, for they represented the security of better times which she felt sure she would never experience again; like the cherished memory of a time and place and person, none of which could ever come together again in the same way, a memory so unique that it is stored not only in the head, but in the heart as well.

She moved toward the telephone, deciding on the way that she would call the taxi first. When she was safe in her room away from the house, she would make the other calls. Maybe by that time Don would be home ... maybe. How odd the house looked with all the lights on, as if she were expecting guests for a large party. Everything looked unnatural in the bright light. There were no shadows. It was like being in a hospital: sterile, impersonal, expectant.

Sally moved through the rooms to the phone as if she were in a dream. Nothing was real to her, nothing had any meaning. If she had seen her husband coming through the door she would not have realized who he was. He could have just been another piece of furniture, another intruder in her fear. But the phone was real enough when she picked it up. It was cold and hard, a clumsy instrument in her hands. It made Sally wish that she were wearing gloves. She wondered if Abner Sloane had ever touched it. Had it been there when he was?

Thinking this, Sally felt a wave of disgust spreading across her fine features. She put the receiver to her ear and waited for the dial tone. There was nothing. It was an odd sensation to expect the familiar tone and to find it gone. Nothing had replaced the sound, no hum, no metallic clicking ... nothing. Even a seashell produced a sound similar to the ocean surf. This was utterly dead.

It took Sally several minutes before she realized that it would not work. They were minutes of frantic manipulation; she hoped desperately that the disorder was only temporary, that some mechanism inside might be stimulated and the telephone would work again. Outside the wind whipped around the house, tearing at the shingles, prying them up then slapping them back down. The rain rushed through the gutters, spilling over the edges and cascading down the sides of the house. She still expected to see the face at the window.

Sally stood terrified, holding the phone in her hand. The storm had broken down the lines and she was unable to call anyone, even a stranger. Why had there been a storm that night, when it had been clear and springlike for days? Why *then?* Was everything in nature against her? Was everything conspiring to help her toward her awful destiny? It seemed the only answer ... unless. Unless the storm was helped by someone.

The thought streaked across her mind so fast that she hardly had time to recognize it before she knew it must be the truth. It couldn't just be chance that had worked against her. No, there had to be a "personal" factor behind it. The same factor that had arranged for her to be in the cellar and to be in the living room in the middle of the night had once again maneuvered things to his advantage. How much more helpless could she be than at that moment? She tried to think. There was no way she could get help, no one she could run to. Nothing.

A sound pricked her ears. It came from the kitchen. It rose above the sound of the storm like a plaintive cry for help, yet there were no words. She had heard it before; low, moaning, a sound ripped from a tormented soul. It was the same sound that had called her to come for the ring. The same sound that had started the cycle of terror. The same sound.

Abruptly, without realizing what she was doing, she was screaming, her voice filled the air with panic. "Stop it! For God's sake stop it!" The sound continued. Then, with almost a sense of gratitude, she felt things slipping away from her, going black, and she knew that her troubled mind could take no more. With a sigh that was almost relief, she fainted.

# TEN

When Sally regained consciousness half an hour later the moaning had not stopped. It persisted to remind her that she had an appointment to keep. An appointment similar to the one Alison O'Keefe had kept twenty years before. If she died, there would be no record for anyone to read. She would only be a memory to the people she had known, and when they died she would no longer exist.

But suddenly she was determined that she would not die. She would not let outside forces decide her fate, not when she had something to say about it. With a supreme effort, Sally dragged herself up from the floor and straightened her dress. Everything seemed to be just as she had last left it, nothing had changed. Nothing except the addition of the voice from the other room.

Before she went into the kitchen to get a knife from the pantry she tried the telephone again. It was still dead, and rather than making her frightened, it made her angry. Someone was tampering with the very basics of her life and she would not put up with it. In the kitchen she immediately noticed that the door to the cellar was ajar. Had she overlooked it on her rounds? Not likely. Then she saw that the heavy iron bolt which had locked it had been removed. The place where it had been, was unpainted, exposed-looking in the midst of layer after layer of old paint. The noise came from the cellar.

In the pantry she opened the utensil drawer and selected the largest knife she could find from her bridal set of cutlery. Its blade was heavy and sharply triangular, dull metal at the top and finely honed on the edge. It was as sharp as a razor. She looked at it as if she had never seen it before, turning it over and over in her hands, wondering if she would have to use it on someone ... wondering who that person might be.

There was a glint in her eye that might have been mistaken for madness, but it was not. It was determination and fortitude, for this was her crisis and she was tired of it, so tired that she knew if she failed she would welcome death in whatever form it came. Strange how just a few months before, Sally had wished that she and Don could live forever, go on through life unscathed, while others wrinkled and died. But now she was used to the idea that it could never be that way for anyone else, or herself.

The sound from the basement intensified. It was calling her and she knew it. Gripping the handle of the knife firmly, she left the pantry and walked to the cellar door. When she opened it, there was no sound. She expected it to creak and groan, to complete the scene and announce that she was coming; but there was nothing. It swung easily on its hinges, effortlessly gliding into the kitchen and resting against the wall. She stood at the top of the stairs, staring down into the darkness below.

Suddenly, without warning, the lights in the house went out. It was such a shock that it hurt her eyes and she rubbed them furiously, as if to try to rub the darkness out of them. For a minute she was disoriented. She swayed back and forth, afraid that she would lose her balance. The hand holding the knife trembled with small, almost delicate spasms. Now that it was dark she could see that there was a faint light from the basement. Not the light of a bulb, but from something else, something dim and fluttering. It emitted a dirty, yellowish glow that made the darkness brown and ugly. A sharp, sweet odor reached her nose, and she realized that it was the smell of burning wax; candles had been lit in the cellar.

Sally lifted her shoulders as if in a shrug. Mentally she gathered all her courage and strength and forced herself to move forward. She took a step down; the boards creaked under her feet. For a second the noise from the lower room abated; they had heard her. Another step. And another. Her hands were sweating profusely and she feared the knife would slip from her grip. There was the oddest sensation that she herself was still at the top of the stairs watching her body walking down. She felt as if she could run for help, fly through the air, while this horrible situation was happening to the physical part of her. If she were in a movie there would be a jump cut and she would be through with whatever was to happen. The heroine walks down the stairs to meet her tormentors. There is a scream. And suddenly it's two hours later and the heroine is in the arms of the hero, crying her heart out and holding on to him for dear life. But that was fantasy. This was real.

The smell of the candles was overpowering. Mingled with it was a much more subtle fragrance of spices and flower petals. It was incense, and the clouds of it hung thick over the room, smoky and pervasive in the faint light. The scene was set. All that was now required was some action, some actors, a script and a director. Actually they were all there; only Sally was ignorant of what was about to be played out . . . and she was the star.

Near the bottom of the stairs she halted and turned to look behind her. She didn't expect someone to have followed her down the stairs; that would have been too mundane, too obvious. She did, however, feel that the door might have mysteriously closed behind her: the frosting on the cake. But now that her eyes were accustomed to the dark she could see that the door was still open.

She was about to continue when her eyes rested on the altar at the back of the room. She could see it plainly through the open stairway. What had once appeared as a pile of rocks to her now seemed more obviously constructed. There were two massive stone supports, spaced about seven feet apart but fairly low, on which rested another stone which served as the top, the workspace, of the altar. The entire top of the structure was covered with thick, black candles of various heights burning slowly and casting the unearthly light in which the room was bathed. Hanging above this altar, just visible in the half-light, hung a crucifix—upside down. Sally drew in a short, sharp breath. She had read that this blasphemous practice was usual with Satanic cults. But it was still a great shock to find herself in the middle of one.

There was a slight movement from behind the altar. It was the same place where she had seen the hooded figure the first time. But now she was slightly blinded by the glare from the flames and she couldn't be sure that there had actually been anything there. Still, to be on the safe side, she decided to be cautious when she got that far ... if she got that far. It was also from this end of the room that the sounds were coming. That awful, grating moaning and howling which had called to her once before. If only that would stop, she could collect herself enough to go on. But perhaps that was the point of the sound, to put her off her guard, to make her feel so insecure that she would not notice other things which she otherwise might.

She walked the rest of the way into the cellar. It was damp down there, more damp than she remembered. But then there had been no storm, no rain seeping into the house driven by the winds. It truly felt like a cellar now; cold and clammy—like the hand of a corpse. She could imagine the walls covered with slimy green moss or mold, growing ceaselessly in this climate of death and decay. The thought made her shiver more than the temperature did.

Turning now to face the altar at the back of the room, Sally saw that the faint outlines of the pentangle which she had noticed before on the floor of the basement had been gone over with white paint. It now stood out clearly, and at each apex of the figure a candle had been placed. In its center a brazier of what appeared to be copper stood fueled, but not fired. She shook her head in wonder. She knew enough about these rites to know that this one was all set up, was waiting and perfect in its own way. Whoever had gone to all this trouble knew what he—or she—was doing. There were no two ways about it.

A voice, soft and crooning, called out to her. "You wear the ring. You shall be His and He shall be ours." It came from near the altar. Whether it was the voice of a man or a woman the young girl could not tell. There was something familiar about it, but she wasn't sure. She wasn't sure that she could tell the voice of her best friend in a situation like this.

"You wear the ring and you shall be His. He shall be ours," another voice said. This one was more recognizable as a man. But what man? She knew so few people in the village that these could be strangers calling her. Why then did she try to recognize the voices? Was it important that these be people she knew? Would it make more sense if these were people she knew rather than strangers?

"You wear the ring. You shall be His and He shall be ours." Again. Again and again. It was worse than the guttural wordless sounds.

In a fit of anger and frustration, Sally called out to the darkness. "I do not wear the ring. I threw it away. Now, who shall be His? You or me?" Her voice rose above the sounds of the storm like a siren wailing in the night. The air was charged with violent emotions. Now they were all pouring forth in a torrent, filling the cellar with an ungodly sound which cut into every crevice of the weathered stone walls.

When she had finished there was a charged and hostile silence. Sally could almost see the faces of the people in the dark as they heard her words. If she no longer wore the ring then the spell, the carefully constructed plot would crumble ... or would it? These people were obviously desperate. They would stop at nothing. There was no reason to suppose that something as simple as not having the ring could keep them away from her.

She walked slowly toward the altar, straining her eyes to see in the strange light. Surely there were figures there in the darkness, she could feel their presence. And then, suddenly, as she drew closer, she could see them. There were three of them behind the altar. All three were dressed exactly as the creature she had encountered on two separate occasions: black cloaks with long, pointed hoods covering their heads and hiding their faces. Three of them. Three people waiting in her house for her to go to them and offer herself as their sacrifice. A sacrifice to the memory of a man who, twenty years before, had killed himself in that very basement after murdering the innocent woman he had employed.

Sally was very aware of the heavy knife in her hand. It weighed on her physical being as heavily as the scene she was playing weighed on her mind. In her mind's eye she could see the shining blade with its thin, mean edge. It was her only friend now, and she knew that if she needed it it would not fail her. Her footsteps echoed in her mind as she crossed the floor toward the horrible altar and its candles. Although she made no sound, she could hear every movement she made, every rustle of her dress, every intake of air into her body. Her skin crawled with tension and a strange kind of excitement. What would happen next?

She passed by the stairs, which were on her left, and moved toward the back of the room. The three figures were silent now, watching her approach. She wondered if they thought she was helpless, a lamb on its way to the slaughter. If they did, then they obviously had no idea how her mind worked, what kind of a woman she was. Could they possibly think that she would allow herself to walk into this situation unarmed? Fools!

Sally was about to speak when she heard a sound from behind her, to the right, by the stairs. She whirled around and saw another figure—a fourth dressed the same as the others—step from the shadows. He had been crouching under the stairs all the while so she hadn't seen him. Whoever these people were, they weren't taking any chances that she would get away. This figure moved into action and lunged forward, arms extended. Sally moved just as quickly, bringing the knife out from the folds of her dress and plunging it deep into the material of her assailant's cloak. He stopped for a second, then yelled in pain and fear. Sally pulled the knife back and saw the thick, dark blood smeared along the blade. Her head reeled.

The man threw his head back in pain and as he did, the hood which had been covering his face fell onto his shoulders. For a second Sally couldn't believe her eyes. She was looking into the face of her husband seconds before he died, a thick trickle of blood streaming from the corners of his mouth. For one second their eyes met and suddenly everything was clear to her. Suddenly she understood everything.

He fell to the floor with a crash and Sally dropped the knife. From behind her she heard the sounds of running feet. There was nothing she could do now. Nothing she wanted to do. Her life was over. With a sob wrenched from her soul, she fell to the floor next to the inert figure of her husband.

# ELEVEN

Sally slowly opened her eyes, trying to remember what had happened to her. She was lying down, and when she tried to move she found that she couldn't. She was bound by her arms and her feet, and every movement she made was painful. Lifting her head slightly, she saw that thick cords pinioned her to the floor of the cellar, allowing only a minimum of movement. It came as a shock to her that she should be in this position; it was also a greater shock when she discovered that she was naked.

The floor of the cellar was like ice; cold and wet. It was almost painful to have her bare skin touching the stone, but when she tried to move to keep the circulation going, the ropes cut into her. Giving up her struggle for the moment, she closed her eyes and hoped that somehow she would get free. What had happened to her? How had she got into this position?

As if flood gates had been opened, the memories came rushing back to her all at once: the diary, the music, the lights going out ... and Don. It must have all been a dream. Her husband couldn't be dead—killed by her own hand. No, she had talked with his secretary earlier. He was probably out looking at that apartment he had talked of. And, if that were true, then how could he have been in the cellar when she walked down the stairs. How could his body have been penetrated by the cold, merciless carving knife? How could his blood have drenched the floor next to her?

There were sounds from above her. Someone was walking around upstairs. It must be Don, she thought. He must have come home. He will see the open door and he'll be down here any minute to free me from these bonds. She listened closely to the sounds. There was more than one person up there—at least two. Who could Don be with? Someone from the city? Evelyn Henderson? Her mind screamed out, "Why don't you come down here and get me. I'm cold and afraid."

The room was still full of the dirty light from the candles. More seemed to have been lighted, for the place where Sally lay was now alive with flickering tongues of flame. She lifted her head and looked around. The brazier which had been set in the center of the mystical pentangle was against the far wall, still ready for a fire. It had been moved to make room for something more important, something more special—Sally herself. With extreme horror the young woman discovered that she had been bound into its center, one extremity tied to each point, her head resting on the last. She was the sacrifice.

Voices, soft and whispering, floated down from the upstairs rooms. One of them, a woman's, was harsh and strident, piercing the calm of the other. Two other voices apparently tried to soothe the third one.

They were caressing and gentle, softening the anger of their compatriot. Sally tried to make out the words that were being spoken, words which she knew had nothing to do with her rescue, but had to do with her death. But from where she was she could make out nothing at all, nothing but the sounds, the rise and fall of the voices, their intonation and passion.

At long last she heard footsteps getting closer to the cellar door. It must have been shut, for now the latch clicked ominously as it opened. A thick shaft of light cut through the gloom of the basement, like a beam of sunshine breaking through storm clouds; only this time it was not a hopeful sign, it indicated that Sally's fate was about to commence.

The footsteps on the stairs were heavy and foreboding. They were evenly paced, rhythmic and insistent—like the sound of dripping water. From where she was tied, Sally could only see her tormentors from their feet to their knees, and they all looked the same in their robes. When the last one left her line of sight, she knew that they were all down with her, all standing behind her, watching. She felt embarrassed because of her nakedness and scared for her life.

The procession moved around her and stood at her feet. She could see now that there were three of them, all dressed as she had expected, in the costume she had come to know. Each one of them held an enormous black candle at waist level and their faces were obscured by the halo of light from the candle flame. There were no sounds now ... nothing but heavy silence. From the tilt of their hoods, Sally could tell that they were watching her. What is going on in their minds? she wondered. What do they have planned for me now that I have killed one of their number?

Killed. Had she really killed someone. Wasn't it just part of the horrible dream she was having? She could never kill anyone. She hated to even kill a fly or a mosquito in the summer, for it made her feel bad for minutes afterward. And to kill a human being, that was out of the question. Even television Westerns made her nervous and vaguely sick. She could never kill anyone. Yet she knew that she had. And that knowledge made her feel like an animal, a savage, a creature beneath contempt. But she had had to protect herself. It was the law of the jungle. And for the first time since she and her husband had moved into the house, she realized what she had thought of the dead forests surrounding it: a jungle, a sick, malignant jungle, from which there was no escape.

The three figures moved, putting their candles down in front of them, anchoring them securely on the floor. Then, one by one, they threw back their hoods so Sally could see their faces. She was not at all surprised when she saw Evelyn Henderson and her husband Ralph. Nor was she really amazed to find that the third was Silas Dorn, the realtor who had been so kind about finding them the house. And now, of course, she knew that Don would never be coming home to her again. He was home for good and would never leave.

Evelyn's face was a mask of hatred. Her teeth were clenched tightly together and when she spoke, her mouth hardly moved. "You have killed our brother and you will die for it."

Sally lifted her head and laughed. "What difference does it make? I was going to die long before I killed him." She spoke of her husband as if she had never known him, as if he had really been a stranger. And, when she thought about it, she realized that he *had been* a stranger; she had not known anything about him.

Evelyn stepped closer. "You will die slowly and painfully. I will see to that. If it hadn't been for you, he would still be alive, still be able to be here to watch the ultimate sacrifice. He waited twenty years for this, and now..." Her eyes drifted off toward the staircase.

Sally's gaze followed them, and under the stairs she saw a body lying on its side, legs pulled up, arms outstretched. It was all that remained of her loving husband, who had taken her from the city, brought her to this house, and participated as she was tortured by these people. It had all been a monstrous plan to get her into the house and keep her there until the anniversary of Sloane's death.

Ralph Henderson leaned forward and touched the sleeve of his wife's robe. "We'd better get on with it, Evelyn. It's nearly time." He was as timid as he had always been. The woman made no move. Her eyes went back to Sally and stayed there.

"Ralph's right," Dorn said. "It is getting late and we don't want anything to go wrong." He smiled evilly at Sally, leering at her nakedness.

Something from Alison's diary came back to the trapped girl. Alison had seen someone from the village at the blasphemous ceremonies in the woods. Could it have been that Silas Dorn was that person? That of course would explain a lot of things: why Don was so friendly with him from the outset, why the house had come so cheap, and why Silas was there now.

Evelyn's eyes burned brightly. "Light the fire," she commanded, "we're ready to begin." She walked back to the altar, where she picked up an enormous book, then she returned to her original position. "You are such a fool, Sally. Such a fool," she said, before opening the book.

In the background Ralph went over to the brazier and put a match to it. Immediately, it burst into flames, sending clouds of gray smoke into the confined space of the basement. The smell reached Sally's nostrils and she choked, gasping for air. It didn't seem to bother any of the others. They must be used to it, Sally thought rather bemusedly, from other sacrifices. The flames leaped from the copper basin as if they were trying to reach the ceiling to set the rest of the house on fire.

Evelyn had begun to read from the book. She spoke loudly and clearly as she called on Satan and all his disciples to present themselves at this sacrifice in Satan's honor. The litany was long and tedious and the language so obscene and blasphemous that Sally could hardly bear to hear the words. Yet she was fascinated as much as she was repelled. Could they really believe that by cursing all that was good and calling upon all that was bad they could make the Devil manifest himself? Her blood would be spilled for no reason, for she was sure that nothing would happen. Or perhaps they didn't expect any reward in this life, but thought that once they were dead they would assume their proper places in Hell.

The two men read while Evelyn began to chant. Each took a turn reading while the others sang that horrible song—if that's what it was. They rocked to and fro in unison, never taking their eyes off Sally. For her part, Sally would not let them have the satisfaction of seeing her fear, so she stared them in the eyes, making her defiance known.

After a while, Evelyn said, "She is strong. It will have to be slow."

"I told you that when I first met her. Don agreed with me, but he said there were ways to break her down, ways to make her unsure of herself. I trust he was right."

"He may have been right, but he's dead now. Did he expect that to happen too?" Sally's words shrieked out from deep within her, propelled by the outraged knowledge that she had been used by her own husband for this reason. He had known from the hour of their marriage that this day would come. How he must have enjoyed the wait, setting Sally up, making her feel secure. She hated him.

At the sound of the words, Evelyn flew forward and slapped Sally across the face so hard that she lost consciousness for a few seconds. "You will pay for that," she said. "Let's start." She went to the altar again and returned with a long, thin knife, the handle of which was shaped like the head of a goat.

She called on Satan to protect her, and to visit her, then moved forward to the girl on the floor. Sally was no longer frightened. Too much had happened to her in that house in the last few hours for anything like fear to be present now. Now that her death was just inches away she felt nothing. There was nothing to feel.

Evelyn bent over her and put the blade of the knife on Sally's thorax. The metal was cool and reassuring, the point of the blade, a thin finger poking at her. With two quick motions, Evelyn drew the blade deeply across the skin. "His sign," she whispered, her eyes glaring with madness, specks of foam frothing at the corners of her mouth.

The pain didn't start until a few minutes later.

Sally could feel the blood trickling across her breasts and rolling down her sides to pool on the floor. She wondered if her blood was mingling with that of her husband's. There was no way to know. She lay there waiting for Evelyn's next move. But the other woman was in no hurry. She wanted this to be as prolonged and as painful as possible.

At last Evelyn proceeded. She carried a branding iron which had been heating in the brazier. Its blunt, ornate end was red-hot and smoking in the humidity of the basement. Evelyn drew closer, brandishing the iron like a sword. "And now you will taste his fiery tongue." She held the iron over Sally's head and slowly lowered it.

Suddenly, there was a crashing of glass and a sound like an exploding firecracker. Evelyn's eyes rolled upward and she dropped the branding iron on the floor. Her body fell heavily to one side landing on the iron. The room filled with the smell of gun powder and burning cloth and flesh.

# TWELVE

After Evelyn had been shot, Silas Dorn and Ralph Henderson tore off their gowns and raced for the stairs. They got as far as the kitchen before the sounds of breaking wood reached Sally's ears. There was shouting, scuffling, then silence. It seemed an eternity before someone started down the stairs to help her.

She looked up and saw the welcome face of Dr. Simpson. He swiftly cut the cords that bound her, wrapped her in a blanket he had brought with him, and carried her upstairs to the study. As they passed through the kitchen, she saw two policemen holding Ralph Henderson and Silas Dorn. They looked scared.

It didn't take long to tend to her wounds, they were only minor cuts, despite the pain they caused. Simpson was silent the whole time, not looking at Sally, never letting her catch his eye. When he was finished taking care of her wounds, he took her by the hand and led her upstairs to her bedroom. Once she was safe in bed he administered an injection to make her sleep. He left the room quietly and called Mrs. Chambers.

Sally's eyes closed wearily and she drifted off to sleep, her disturbed mind lulled by the injection.

The next morning was bright and cheerful. The sun poured through the windows and the air was sweet from the previous night's rain. Everything was warm and gentle. Sally felt safe for the first time in months. Mrs. Chambers sat next to the bed working on some needlepoint. When she saw that her ward's eyes were open, she put down her work and smiled.

"I don't know how you feel, but you look one hundred times better than when I saw you last night. You scared the heart out of me."

Sally managed to smile weakly. "You've been here since last night?"

"Ever since Dr. Simpson called me and said you needed help. You know I never liked this house. I knew something bad was going to happen, ever since that first time I came to stay with you. You poor dear." She extended her hand and took Sally's.

"Is Dr. Simpson here? I'd like to talk with him."

"He said he'd be by around lunchtime. Speaking of which, are you hungry? It's long past breakfast, but I'll make you anything you want."

Sally thought for a minute, then said: "I would like some tea, that's all. If it's not too much trouble."

Mrs. Chambers frowned. "After what you've been through, nothing will be too much. I'll be back in a minute." She got up from her chair and left the room.

When she returned ten minutes later, Mrs. Chambers was all smiles. "Look who I found lurking downstairs." She stepped aside and let Dr. Simpson enter.

He smiled a great, warm smile and advanced to the

bed. "How are you feeling today? You look a lot better."

"I feel much better, thank you. And thank you for saving my life."

"I'm only glad that I got here in time to help you. I had a flat tire on my way here and I was afraid I might be too late."

Sally accepted the tea, took a sip of the hot beverage and said: "How did you know that they were going to come after me last night? In fact, how did you know anything at all?"

Simpson looked from Sally to Mrs. Chambers then back again. "I think we had better leave the questions and answers to later. You need a lot of rest. You've been through something that most people could never recover from."

Sally lifted herself up on her elbows. "I need to know what happened. You have to understand how important it is that *I* understand. Remember, last night I lost my husband . . . I killed him. You can't just let me go on in ignorance." Tears were welling up in her eyes and she felt a tenseness coil up inside her.

"I don't think it's a good idea, but if you insist, I'll tell you. At the beginning, I thought that you were just hysterical. I thought that maybe you had had a fight with your husband and wanted attention. Frankly, the story about seeing someone in the basement was preposterous, or so it seemed. But then there was the second incident. Your reactions were too strong, too violent to have been just imagination. And when I found the ring on your finger I had no other choice but to believe what you had said. It was at that point that I decided your life was in danger, but I didn't know why, or who was behind it.

"I took the ring and sent it to my friend, as I told

you. What I didn't tell you was that I learned that the ring was given to victims of a sacrifice before the ceremony to consecrate them. You were clearly marked for death. When you showed me the second ring I had to do some fast work. Evelyn Henderson had said she had found it on the stairway where you had dropped it, but that was impossible because I had the ring all the time, so there was obviously a second ring ... one which she produced. Then there was your husband's reaction when he discovered the ring was gone. All along he had given the impression that you were slightly out of your mind, that he didn't believe that anything had ever happened to you. Yet, when he examined your finger, there was a look of shock when he observed that there was no ring. I wondered about his expression if he hadn't expected something to be there. That seemed to link him with Evelyn Henderson in some way. But I couldn't figure out how.

"I said nothing because I had no proof. And I knew you were safe as long as Mrs. Chambers was here. I started to think about this house and the Henderson place, and how strange it was that after all the years of being derelict this place had suddenly been refurbished and redecorated. Why, after all that time? There had to be a reason. And these houses had both belonged to Abner Sloane and both were now rented out. Who owned them now? They should have gone to his relatives when he died. There were three children, you know. Two boys and a girl. What had become of them?" The doctor paused and looked to see if his story was wearying Sally. She appeared fascinated and alert. He went on.

"I've spent the last few days checking things out. Everything seemed to fit into a plan, an enormous scheme which had started the day you moved in.

There were many pieces to the puzzle, and I had to fit them together before it was too late. Something was going to happen, but when? I had a strong suspicion that it would be soon. It wasn't until last night that I realized that it had been exactly twenty years ago that Sloane had killed himself.

"I had traced down the children of Sloane and once I had done that everything fell into place. After he died, the children were sent off to an orphanage; there were no other relatives. The girl and the eldest boy had been adopted by one family. The other boy by another. Evelyn Henderson and Ralph Henderson are not married; they never were, because their real names are Cynthia and David Sloane. I guess by now you can guess that your husband, Don was the third child, raised by the Taylor family. His real name was Edward Sloane."

Sally had begun to cry, the tears coursing down her cheeks. She had been lied to and cheated all her married life. She had married a monster and had never suspected it. She wished she had died at the hands of Cynthia Sloane.

"I know this is hard on you, but you have to know it—so you can go on. They were sick; you've got to understand that. They were brought up by that man with one goal in life, to serve the Devil. You must try to forget them."

Sally shook her head slowly. "How can I forget them. How can I forget my husband, what he did to me. What can I do?"

The doctor smiled. "You can go on living. These houses are yours now. You can sell them and move back to the city ... or maybe you'll choose to live here. You may find another man to love."

She smiled sadly. "Where? I can never trust anyone again."

He leaned forward and caressed her cheek. "There are *some* people you can trust. Some people who truly care about you. Take me, for example." He smiled.

Sally took his hand from her cheek and held it tightly. Maybe he was right. Maybe she could start over and go on living. Maybe life was not the dark tunnel she was afraid it had become. She smiled at the doctor and wondered what it would be like to be the wife of a country physician.

Novels that present the rich historical tapestry surrounding and detailing the period of the War of the Roses—the bloody struggle between the Houses of York and Lancaster for the throne of England.

| | | |
|---|---|---|
| P00141-X | THE WARRIOR KING, No. 1<br>Brenda Honeyman | .95 |
| P00153-3 | THE ROSE IN SPRING, No. 2<br>Eleanor Fairburn | .95 |
| P00167-3 | THE WARWICK HEIRESS, No. 3<br>Margaret Abbey | .95 |
| P00186-X | SON OF YORK, No. 4 Margaret Abbey | .95 |
| P00198-3 | RICHMOND & ELIZABETH, No. 5<br>Brenda Honeyman | .95 |

and more to come . . .

---

**TO ORDER**
Please check the space next to the book/s you want, send this order form together with your check or money order, include the price of the book/s and 15¢ for handling and mailing to:

PINNACLE BOOKS, INC. / P.O. Box 4347
Grand Central Station / New York, N.Y. 10017

☐ CHECK HERE IF YOU WANT A FREE CATALOG.

I have enclosed $_____ check_____ or money order_____
as payment in full. No C.O.D.'s.

Name_____

Address_____

City_____ State_____ Zip_____
(Please allow time for delivery.)

*History's Most Fascinating Women Series*

# by Maureen Peters

**THE QUEEN WHO NEVER WAS** is the enthralling and unforgettable story of Elizabeth Woodville, whose quest for England's throne was lost in the War of Roses.
P00130-4  95¢

**THE VIRGIN QUEEN** tells the glittering and tempestuous story of Elizabeth Tudor, a woman of power and passion, who overcame every palace intrigue to reign over England's most glorious years.   P00143-6  95¢

**DESTINY'S LADY** is the story of Lady Jane Grey, the extraordinary woman whose beauty and intelligence swept her to the mighty throne of England.
P00177-0  95¢

**PRINCESS OF DESIRE** is the compelling story of Mary-Rose Tudor and her struggle to find love amidst the false and sinister shadows surrounding the throne of England.   P00193-2  95¢

--------

_____P00130-4   THE QUEEN WHO NEVER WAS, No. 1   .95

_____P00143-6   THE VIRGIN QUEEN, No. 2   .95

_____P00177-0   DESTINY'S LADY, No. 3   .95

_____P00193-2   PRINCESS OF DESIRE, No. 4   .95

**more to come . . .**

**TO ORDER**
Please check the space next to the book/s you want, send this order form together with your check or money order, include the price of the book/s and 15¢ for handling and mailing to:
PINNACLE BOOKS, INC. / P.O. Box 4347
Grand Central Station / New York, N. Y. 10017
☐ Check here if you want a free catalog.
I have enclosed $_____check_____or money order_____
as payment in full. No C.O.D.'s.

Name_____

Address_____

City_____State_____Zip_____
(Please allow time for delivery.)

# BRILLIANT NOVELS OF PASSION AND GLORY

## by Anne Powers

**NO WALL SO HIGH** is a stirring novel of passion and intrigue—a national bestseller—finally in paperback! *The Saturday Review* called it "an historical romance on a large scale . . . quick-paced, brimming with dramatic characters." P00188-6   $1.50

**RACHEL** is the story of an exciting woman, perhaps the greatest actress of all time. Her life, her being, only existed for the stage. She survived the hunger, and misery of poverty to live in a Paris that glittered and clamored for those who lived in stardom.
P00216-5   $1.50

**THE ONLY SIN.** In this fast-moving, electrifying saga of foreign mystery, romance and espionage, all the color of 18th century India emerges and blends into a shimmering collage of shadowy secrets and treasures of the East. P00260-2   $1.25

| | | | |
|---|---|---|---|
| _____ | P00188-6 | NO WALL SO HIGH | 1.50 |
| _____ | P00216-5 | RACHEL | 1.50 |
| _____ | P00260-2 | THE ONLY SIN | 1.25 |

**TO ORDER**
Please check the space next to the book/s you want, send this order form together with your check or money order, include the price of the book/s and 15¢ for handling and mailing to:
PINNACLE BOOKS, INC. / P.O. Box 4347
Grand Central Station / New York, N.Y. 10017
☐ Check here if you want a free catalog.
I have enclosed $_____ check_____ or money order_____
as payment in full. No C.O.D.'s.

Name_____

Address_____

City_____ State_____ Zip_____
(Please allow time for delivery.)

# GREAT GOTHIC READING
# FOR THE DISCRIMINATING WOMAN

**THE GREAT STONE HEART, by Mona Farnsworth.** An exciting romance set in old Santa Fe at the turn of the century—the story of a young girl who comes to the colorful desert town to work as a model to a famous sculptress, and finds mystery and death.
 **P022—95¢**

**THE BELLS OF WIDOWS' BAY, by Miriam Lynch.** This richly textured tale takes its heroine, Lisa Meredith, through a web of intrigue, love and betrayal. It is set on a remote island, Widows' Bay, where her fiance has taken her on a weekend's visit. You'll find one climax after another in this exciting story.
 **P049—95¢**

**DUELING OAKS, by Daniella Dorsett.** A whirlwind romance leads Deanna to the altar and an elegant Southern plantation, but the glamour soon turns to terror at the point of her husband's sword. Set in New Orleans right after the Civil War, this suspenseful and romantic novel will enthrall you.
 **P074—95¢**

**WHERE SHADOWS LIE, by Miriam Lynch.** This is the story of Elizabeth Lyman, a lovely New England girl. She is a descendant of an old American Family. The scene is set in a small town just outside of Boston where Elizabeth's great-aunts live in a foreboding mansion, Gray House. Mystery follows mystery in this chilling, yet romantic, novel.
 **P086—95¢**

**BLUE MARSH, by Thelma René Bernard.** Aurelie Martin, a lovely young orphan in search of excitement and romance, is travelling alone, on her way to a new home, when she meets a handsome and wealthy stranger. She's charmed by him, and somehow, becomes involved in a sinister plot. Her dreams of fulfillment and love seem about to be dashed on the rocks of despair . . . when she discovers that there's a way out of her haunted existence. A Pinnacle Great Gothic, in large type, of course.
 **P105—95¢**

**A CROSS FOR TOMORROW, by Mona Farnsworth.** Another Great Pinnacle Gothic, set in large type. Margaret Alden's gone to visit her school friend, Elaine, who has married into an old aristocratic Latin family. The unusual mystique of the place begins to give way to violence . . . and murder. Margaret becomes enmeshed in the rituals of an ancient and secret religious cult known as Penitentes. A strange and mysterious story.
 **P106—95¢**

*To order see page 160*

**NIGHTMARE'S MORNING, by Miriam Lynch.** A new, original large-type Gothic romance—with a bizarre twist. This is the story of Ellen Barclay, a young secretary. She's been hired by an author to aid him in research and manuscript preparation. They are to spend much of their time in an old New England mansion known as Shadowlawn. The mansion is infamous as the site of a brutal multiple murder more than eighty years ago. On the very first day strange things begin to occur, and it is soon apparent that history may be repeating itself. Will murder be next? **P110—95¢**

**STARCROSSED ROAD, by Mona Farnsworth.** Here is an unusual and haunting Gothic novel of suspense, set in modern times, and written by one of our most popular authors. It tells the story of Elizabeth Wainwright, who left her conservative Boston home to travel across the United States to join the strange household of Miranda Field, who lived in Oregon. There were three men living there and two other women—but not a soul she could trust. Chilling romance, from the author of THE GREAT STONE HEART and A CROSS FOR TOMORROW.
**P162—95¢**

**RENDEZVOUS IN PEKING, by Anne-Mariel.** An absorbingly real novel of love and terror—a novel that will transport every reader to the subtle and sensual atmosphere of the Orient. When Marie-Laure, the heroine, attempts to free her husband from Red China, where he is being held on a charge of murdering his first wife, she encounters a world both dream and nightmare. Newly-wed, she learns much about her husband after he is taken from her which both frightens and intrigues her; then she is forced to masquerade as the wife of a Communist Chinese Colonel, with whom she falls in love. **P187—95¢**

**THE EVIL THAT WAITED, by Mona Farnsworth.** After Daphne Partridge's parents were killed in a tragic automobile accident, she was forced to leave the small New England town where she had always lived. In 1904, a young girl of good breeding but no money had little choice except to find a relative who would take her in. She was prepared to work and to accept the customary sympathy. However, she could never have been prepared for the chilling and haunting experiences that awaited her at the home of her distant cousin, Miss Ellen Fairtree. It was a beautiful house, in which there was something ominously threatening, something evil that no one could control. She had entered a nightmare world, and there seemed no way out.
**P00211-4—95¢**

*To order see page 160*

**MOONSHADOW MANSION, by Thelma René Bernard.** An unusual and romantic gothic set in England. When Destiné, a young governess who has been deserted by her only relative, is forced to take a job in a remote manor in the north of England, she finds mystery and despair. Hearing strange noises, Destiné and her young charge begin to explore together. They find more mystery . . . and eventually, death. Frightened as she is, Destiné knows she cannot stop now. She must find out who the murderer is before she, or the child she has grown to love, become victims. The suspense builds to a spine-tingling climax when she finds there are others living in the manor too! **P00222-X—95¢**

**LADY OF LONGING, by Marilyn D. Lynch.** This is a novel of passion and romantic intrigue, an attractive, lonely wife of a POW finds herself hopelessly entangled in an affair with her husband's best friend. It has been several years since Hallie and her young sons have even heard from the missing head of the family. Hallie has reached the throes of desperation when Jase enters her life, offering both love and the security of marriage. Should she succumb? **P00249-1—95¢**

**MY SECRET LOVE, by Dana Brookins.** A young woman of twenty-six, moves to a small town after her ailing mother dies from a prolonged illness. Cara soon falls madly in love with the town preacher, whose wife is in a sanitarium for the insane. The preacher has several children, and the oldest, who is a lonely, alienated figure, seems to suspect the torrid love that is going on around him. One afternoon, while Cara and the preacher are on a Sunday-school picnic, a large boulder mysteriously becomes dislodged and cascades down an embankment, smashing the preacher's hand and killing one of the children! How did the rock fall? Is it possible that someone pushed it? **P00297-1—95¢**

**AFRAID OF THE DARK, by Mary Linn Roby.** Hoping to find some excitement and romance to break up the boredom of her monotonous life, Laura Cassell saves for years for a cruise to Rio de Janeiro. On the eve of her departure, she returns to her Boston apartment to find her brother Justin has been brutally beaten. He tells her that the assailants had actually been waiting there to kill her. They were planning to force him to pay his gambling debts with the money from her life insurance. But if she could get to the ship and out of the country, she would be safe. However, once on shipboard, Laura discovers that she has walked into a far more dangerous trap than the one which she has fled. The first night at sea, someone tries to murder her. There are no witnesses and Laura's story sounds like the attention-seeking fantasy of a hysterical girl. Soon the cruise becomes nothing less than a nightmare of terror and death, as Laura tries in vain to identify her enemy! **P00311-0—95¢**

*To order see page 160*

# This is your Order Form . . .
## Just clip and mail.

| | | |
|---|---|---|
| _____P00022-7 | THE GREAT STONE HEART | .95 |
| _____P00049-9 | THE BELLS OF WIDOW'S BAY | .95 |
| _____P00074-X | DUELING OAKS | .95 |
| _____P00086-3 | WHERE SHADOWS LIE | .95 |
| _____P00105-3 | BLUE MARSH | .95 |
| _____P00106-1 | A CROSS FOR TOMORROW | .95 |
| _____P00110 | NIGHTMARE'S MORNING | .95 |
| _____P00162 | STARCROSSED ROAD | .95 |
| _____P00187 | RENDEZVOUS IN PEKING | .95 |
| _____P00211-4 | THE EVIL THAT WAITED | .95 |
| _____P00222-X | MOONSHADOW MANSION | .95 |
| _____P00249-1 | LADY OF LONGING | .95 |
| _____P00297-1 | MY SECRET LOVE | .95 |
| _____P00311-0 | AFRAID OF THE DARK | .95 |

---

TO ORDER

Please check the space next to the book/s you want, send this order form together with your check or money order, include the price of the book/s and 15¢ for handling and mailing, to:

PINNACLE BOOKS, INC. / P.O. Box 4347
Grand Central Station / New York, N.Y. 10017

☐ Check here if you want a free catalog.

I have enclosed_____check_____or money order_____
as payment in full. No C.O.D.'s.

Name_____

Address_____

City_____ State_____ Zip_____
(Please allow time for delivery.)